Advance Praise

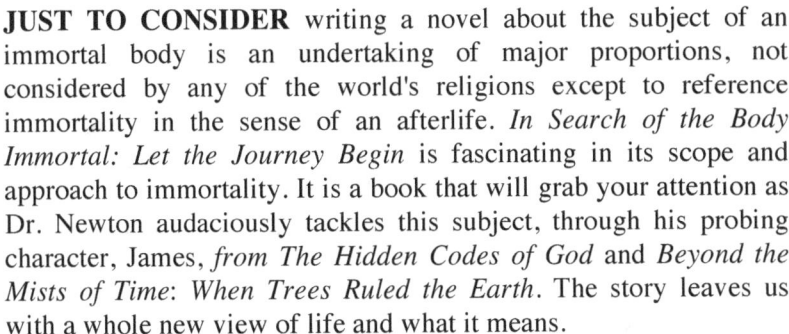

JUST TO CONSIDER writing a novel about the subject of an immortal body is an undertaking of major proportions, not considered by any of the world's religions except to reference immortality in the sense of an afterlife. *In Search of the Body Immortal: Let the Journey Begin* is fascinating in its scope and approach to immortality. It is a book that will grab your attention as Dr. Newton audaciously tackles this subject, through his probing character, James, *from The Hidden Codes of God* and *Beyond the Mists of Time*: *When Trees Ruled the Earth*. The story leaves us with a whole new view of life and what it means.

This most certainly is a book you want to read over and over so as to savor the implications for you personally and the world at large! Although using a fiction approach to deliver a much-needed message and share his passion about immortality, this wonderfully prolific writer also makes the connection, and gives you cause to take a new perspective of, health and disease as well.

~ Bertha Nash,
Health Care Provider
Compassionate Care by Bertha Nash

IMMORTALITY... I HAVE come to this point in life knowing two things to be certain: we are born and we then die. Myriad people have been passionate about wanting to cheat death, such as Billionaire Dmitry Itskov in his initiative to create artificial bodies to house human intelligence, and LifeNaut's proposed use of mind-files to reconstruct ourselves somewhere in the future.

i

Another certainty... immortality is not a quest on which only those of us in the 21st century focus; there is evidence as far back as the third century B.C., when Chinese Emperor Qin Shi Huang ingested mercury to gain eternal life. In the 1980's we read of Wade Davis, who documented cases of the Haitian dead rising from their graves. The world over, for time eternal, people have conceived of many processes and inventions to extend human life. None of these concepts are without controversy.

Robert Newton has challenged this controversy in a unique novel, *In Search of the Body Immortal: Let the Journey Begin*, which is both entertaining and highly thought provoking. The conversations between James, the character Dr. Newton has evolved through a series of other novels, and his deceased wife, Ann, can do no less than take us beyond the reality of statistics about Americans. For example, statistics suggest that by 2030 the number of Americans older than 65 will have grown by roughly 75%. This fact alone gives us reason to consider what some may view as lofty ideas to prevent aging and physical deterioration. Newton stays away from the financial and political stances, staying comfortably within the realms of spiritual growth that has been his life journey. With equal parts of brilliance and idealism, the author is adamant immortality is congruent with the growing interest in solving life's ultimate problem, which just happens to be death.

Wrinkle creams and hair re-growth is not what the author seeks to convey, nor is the demographic force that drives a market for mortality to the field—a field that is anticipated to surge to roughly $20 billion over the next decade! Newton brilliantly addresses the reality that before we can begin to approach mortality, it is our personal responsibility to manage the "stuff" that kills us! The message in this story is clear: managing our health naturally, spiritually, and nutritionally is foundational to the ultimate quest of immortality.

~ TR Stearns
Editor, Former Educator,
and Superintendent of Schools

SO MUCH THOUGHT provoking and life changing information is herein to be had for the studious reader. Learning and seeking to understand, as I have, can literally change your life as my own has been changed and transformed. Discovering Pranayama Breathwork for Theta Healing and various other teachings from the renowned Dr. Newton empowered me to 'Go to White' once I face a life or death crisis.

Take in the information and dig deeper into the roots of the meaning of words.

Mem Bet Hey: Thought into Action

Vav Hey Vav: Happiness

Mem Yud Hey: Unity

Ayin Shin Lamed: Global Transformation begins in your own Heart;

Now, discover for yourself: *Pey Vav Yud*; *Ayin Resh Yud*; and Yud Yud Yud   .

~ David Herold Roscher
C.HT, Advanced Psych-K Facilitator,
Lifestyle Strategist + Custom Solutions Specialist;
https://about.me/dynamicdavid

In Search of the Body Immortal

Let the Journey Begin

In Search of the Body Immortal

Let the Journey Begin

By

Robert J. Newton, J.D., N.D

Great Motivational Talks
ISBN- **9780996137140**
ISBN- **0996137149**

Dr. Robert J. Newton

Beyond the Bounds of Earth Publishing,
Entertainment and Education

20253 Evening Breeze Dr.
Walnut, California 91789

http://www.drrobertnewton.com/

Ordering Information:
Quantity sales. Special discounts are available on quantity purchases by corporations, associations, and others. For details, contact the publisher at the address above.

Printed in the United States of America

First Edition

14 13 12 11 10 / 10 9 8 7 6 5 4 3 2 1

Dedication

THIS BOOK IS dedicated to you if you are someone who:

Has such an intense thirst to know and understand God you will overcome any obstacle put in the path of your pursuit.

Always question everything; yet remain pliable enough to accept new information that might be contrary to what you have already learned.

Do not necessarily understand something when it is presented to you, but wisely suspend judgment until you can ascertain the accuracy thereof.

Is never reticent to ask for scientific and annotated proof of what someone presented to you, especially those who ask you to accept something on blind belief.

Knows as certitude you can accomplish anything when you put your thoughts, energy, and powers of visualization toward accomplishing your goal.

Lives by the maxim, "The fool didn't know it couldn't be done, so he went ahead and did it anyway."

Can embrace the reality that many novels are written in such a manner as to entertain the reader, whilst planting new seeds of thought.

Table of Contents

Acknowledgements

A WRITER IS only as good as his sources, his personal connection to other worldly sources such as the Akashic Records, and his imagination and creativity! Herein, I choose to acknowledge the personal sources, each of who helped me to finish a more complete book.

Charlette Ann Smith, deceased, was my wife of thirty-seven years and was my main source and inspiration that brought this book to fruition. Her knowledge of Kriya Kundalini Yoga, Hinduism and Sanskrit mantras was unparalleled on planet Earth and she constantly gave me information and inspiration in my writings.

Cindy Cardenas shared with Charlette and me the Dr. Paul Foster Case Builders of the Adytum (BOTA) information, including *The Emerald Tablets of Hermes Trismegustis*, Dr. Case's *The Pattern on the Trestle Board* and *The 72 Names of God*, from Exodus, in *The Torah*.

Dr. Paul Foster Case was a Renaissance Man, and infused with much esoteric and alchemical knowledge and one of his books is *The Spiritual Keys of Alchemy*. Whenever you go into the land of creating an immortal body, it is helpful if you do so in the context of alchemy.

Yogi Marshall Govindan Satchidananda initiated me into the highest levels of Kriya Kundalini Yoga. Kriya Kundalini Yoga has directly enhanced my awareness of the increased light factor in my body, and my ability to channel the creative process and solve problems.

Bertha Eloina Nash has helped me manage my day-to-day affairs. Possibly too often she is a "writers widow."

Prologue

JAMES' QUEST FOR immortality first began when he was fifteen and introduced to the Science of Christianity, from which point he remained in a life quest for more information about how a body could be immortalized. After his wife Ann, passed on, from a most gruesome death, James became obsessed with finding how he could immortalize his body... more in a state of light rather than the normal state of matter. *In Search of the Body Immortal: Let the Journey Begin*, James comes to this novel, experiencing the awareness there seem to be two things in life about which everyone wants to know.

The first being whether God, as a Creator, even exists. The topic was covered comprehensively in James' explorations in *Pathways to God: Experiencing the Energies of the Everyday God in Your Everyday Life, A Map to Healing and Your Essential Divinity Through Theta Consciousness: Physics of the Immortal Light Body, The Creator's Template of Perfection and Abundance for His People,* and *The Hidden Codes God.*

Within the previous stories of the ever-evolving character, James, ample proof exists that there is a controlling force in this Universe, with immeasurable amounts of perfect geometric forms and all kinds of perfect waveforms on the atomic level of creation. These perfect atomic forms and the very tight parameters, by which life even exists on planet Earth, are strong evidence indicating the presence of a Controlling Force, a Creator; a God!

The second question James is convinced people want to know is whether their life continues after they die, pass on, or leave the good Planet Earth. The topic is prevalent in *Beyond the Mists of Time: When Trees Ruled the Earth,* rich with discussions of how very ancient civilizations actually transcended death and transitioned into a body immortal.

Which now brings us to *In Search of the Body Immortal: Let the Journey Begin*. Here we find James, the character readers loved in *The Hidden Codes of God* and *Beyond the Mists of Time: When Trees Ruled the Earth*, going on his ultimate life mission, in a search of epic proportions, uncovering information in the most unlikely places, of how to immortalize his body. We find James being aided by his deceased wife, Ann, his counterpart in previous novels.

CHAPTER ONE

Incarnating Through The Uterus/Vaginal Vortex And Other Vortexes Of Light

———— ❧ ————

THE OLDER JAMES became, and with the ensuing spiritual and scientific insights he garnered, the more he knew Earth's problems could be solved and replaced with a Heaven on Earth! Where others saw only hell on Earth, or at best, a highly dysfunctional planet, he knew there was an underlying perfection to everything here, as per *Aleph Kaf Aleph, the seventh Name of God from Exodus in *The Torah*. The fact so few people could comprehend this, including people of all faiths and persuasions, did not diminish the validity of James' insights he garnered in studying *The 72 Names of God* in the Judaic text, which revealed to him major insights into the nature of reality on Earth! We could likewise say the nature of our personal reality!

DNA of the Soul – to bring order into your life by connecting to your soul.
http://blueiris.org/community/index.php?option=com_content&view=article&id=516

There were several things James comprehended about why this perfection of things was not seen on Earth. First, you had a *The Torah*, *The Bible* and *The Koran*, which promulgated incessantly, the idea of an imperfect man and an imperfect Earth. With the mishaps that are conjured up by mis-programmed human mind, calamities and sin will inevitably be manifested because the energy from the thoughts behind these concepts cause them to be materialized! Secondly, industries and service providers make money from the mishaps, which have been "programmed" into existence, so certainly they have no vested interest in "setting the record straight," as per Aleph Kaf Aleph, revealing an inherent perfection to everything in the manifestations of God/Creator! Also related to this, the Allopathic medical monopoly, controlled by doctors, hospitals and pharmaceutical companies, make obscene amounts of money from people becoming—and remaining—sick and diseased! Clearly, a diabolical matrix has been created—making us believe we will inevitably deteriorate, need medical intervention and then eventually die. Due to incorrect religious dogma and the ensnaring matrix cannibalizing our personal economic wealth/resources, we become trapped in a false spider web of beliefs and the actions of others who leech away our assets, with no real benefit for us in the long run and even very little—if any—in the near term!

The process of trying to get to what the real nature of things and ourselves in fact are... and whether there really is a perfection on Earth, in the scheme of things, James came across the most propitious information in an internet search, namely, *Geometry of a Uniform Field*! This treatise, by Valery P. Kondratov, discussed and displayed the recurring nine geometric forms of creation on the atomic level. It was easy to see these forms being replicated with a haunting regularity and James clearly realized they are the substructure/foundation of all manifested forms on Earth! All of this was observable in pictures taken with helium ion microscope of platinum crystals.

When James saw the platinum crystals picture, it confirmed the many hunches he had about this in his meditations and dreams and during numerous Kundalini energy infusions/awakenings!

James was fully aware the image was of Platinum Crystals—shown via helium ion microscope. He instantly recalled the nine geometric forms of creation from the *Geometry of a Uniform Field*. These geometric forms are the perfect sub-structure of all creation. The picture was the one by Dr. Erwin

Mueller, circa 1953, where the colored lines were used to emphasize the geometric forms!

As James allowed his mind to focus on the imagery, he further learned about a controlling intelligence, be it God, Creator or Intelligent Design, guiding this perfect creation in Dr. Hugh Ross' *Origins of the Universe*. Dr. Ross explained the very tight parameters within which things operate and exist, especially in regard to a strong Nuclear Force and the Earth's electromagnetic field. The fact that life could only exist within the tight parameters of .003 of one percent in regard to the two fields mentioned, as Dr. Ross revealed in his book, provided James evidence that proves there is indeed an intelligent design to the Earth.

Additionally, fractal geometries are revealed throughout the plant kingdom in vegetables, fruits, plants and trees; they reveal an overwhelming evidence of recurring perfect geometric forms, despite the proclamations of those promoting the concept of Chaos Theory, which is a field of mathematics regarding the behavior of dynamical systems which are commonly found sensitive to initial conditions, such as a response popularly known as the butterfly effect. Indeed, these things were well chronicled in a book James co-authored with Dr. Robert J. Newton, *A Map to Healing and Your Essential Divinity Through Theta Consciousness,* and the previously mentioned book by Valery P. Kondratov, *Geometry of a Uniform Field.*

In his solitude, James contemplated: *If there is this perfection to all creation on the atomic level, it should naturally extend to the perfection of all forms on Earth! It should also definitely extend to the perfection of the human body!* He had come to fervently believe there are undoubtedly systems created for the body, which work with stunning ingenuity and precision, like the various glands, the brain and the autonomic nervous system. Within this context, the human body should never perish from any outside influences, other than the will of the person involved or Acts of God, assuming God even intervenes in a manner to shorten our life spans and that is a huge assumption, in and of itself! Beyond this, as Dr. Deepak Chopra points out in *War of the World Views*, there is no reason why our cells should die, even though they do. The fact these cells are replaced is amazing, in and of itself, but since the atoms that comprise the cells do not expire, why are the cells expiring? James shuddered. Aware of an extremely strong intuition hunch, which had to do with the belief in our eventual demise, as an undeniable fact, feeling he would soon find out why.

Actually, there was a real purpose to James' fringe thinking, although some might even call it "farfetched" and really at the essence of what he was considering, there was ample evidence to take his ideas on immortalizing the human body out of the realm of fringe and shift it into the arena of scientific proof! His breathing became labored as he further realized, undoubtedly, his vision to re-establish a "Heaven on Earth" and have things restored to their perfect state would only be realized if people lived to the long life spans chronicled in *The Torah*. His mind raced, searching for the supporting knowledge that such life spans were actually exhibited in the nine hundred to almost a thousand year life times chronicled in the lives of Adam, Noah, Moses, Jared, Seth, Enos, Cainan, Mahalaleel, Lamech, Nahor, Aphaxa, Methuselah and Enoch, who actually went into a state of physical immortality, aided by Arc Angel Michael. Myriad documents revealed, that not without almost equal standing, Eben lived into his late 800's, and other millennial type life spans were also discovered by Zechariah Sitchin in his twelve books, including *The Cosmic Code* and *Genesis Revisited*, about the Anunaki Civilization from Nibiru/Mardoc when they lived on Earth in Sumer, which are better known as very ancient Iraq and Iran, and other places like Egypt and Atlantis.

James could feel his mind spin almost out of control as he queried why these personages had the capacity to live for such a long span as opposed the puny life spans of humans today. The words reverberated like tones from the carillon in the local church tower as he thought: *This is a big question and a real damn big one to wit!*

Some people believe man's lifespan started diminishing after the Great Flood of Noah, ten to twelve thousand years ago, which was supposedly to cleanse the Earth of the sins of Adam. Others claim the shorter life spans are the result of different atmospheric conditions on Earth. James considered perhaps better answers could lie in the possibility the above named Biblical personages were either extra terrestrial beings or human-extra terrestrial hybrid beings, the result of ET and human mating. Additionally, his brain burned with a belief in some evidence the Anunaki extra terrestrials being referred to, had a twelve strand DNA as opposed to our binary pairs DNA, with only two strands!

How can I open others minds to my belief that "genetic markers" of Anunaki DNA have been found in humans, which would also indicate the people of Earth could live at least in a state of quasi-immortality in the same body? While most people would summarily dismiss the fact that an ET race could even exist on Earth, did not concern James. It was mentioned in Genesis of *The Torah* that God shortened our life spans to 120 years; but who was this God? The "God of Gods" or a demi-God/neter-God, such as Enil, leader of the Anunaki on Earth, as Zechariah Sitchin, a Soviet-born American author of a series of books that proposed an explanation for human origins, which involved ancient astronauts?

One question led to another for James, who, since the age of five had experienced diametric opposites in a "punishing God" who would be inimical to the "loving God." Allowing himself to be reminded of that opposition also brought another question to James' mind: *Why are there so few centurions, let alone people living to 120?* In the light of all of this James pondered why it even makes any difference whether he has ET DNA, human-ET hybrid DNA— or just existing binary pairs DNA of the humans of today— as to how long we can live? *Again, this is a huge question with an even huger answer, most likely!*

In his scheme of viewing things, James then segued into considering other things related to his question! In keeping with respect for the knowledge of The Elders in the Native American Indian and Aboriginal peoples, it was always accepted those who had lived the longest were those who were the leaders, and those best suited to make decisions and solve any problems that were confronted, within the tribal/societal structure! James focused for some time on some of the very insightful indigenous peoples, such as The Lakota and The Cherokee, who used the forces of nature and natural law to guide them in everything they did and as a foundation

5

of knowledge and life guidance. James accepted such as self evident, although that sentiment was not in vogue among the most of the souls living in twenty first century Earth. However, James' perspective of things drew him inextricably to the conclusion: For the problems on Earth to be solved, there needs to be Elders; souls seasoned and wizened over time, as revealed in *The Torah, Gnostic Christian texts, The Mahabarata, The Tibetan Book of the Dead, The Egyptian Book of the* Dead and other tribal and aboriginal teaching based on nature and natural law!

The crucial need to draw this conclusion was only too evident for James in his own life, as far as being able to function with a high level of knowledge and spiritual insight, which just barely began at the age of thirty five and became more evident after his eye opening adventure to Egypt when he was thirty eight. It is this thirty five year old milestone, which many numerologists believe is the drop-dead time at which a person can access the opportunity to attain a high level of spiritual enlightenment in a particular lifetime! While this is not a hard and fast rule, things generally manifest within these accepted Numerological parameters.

Looking back, James did not even think he was really a complex problem solver until he wrote his first book, *Pathways to God: Experiencing the Energies of the Living God in Your Everyday Life,* at the age of forty-four, with Dr. Robert Newton. For James, intelligence, while useful and necessary, was the least of all beneficial components when compared to **wisdom**, which could be considered **applied/functional knowledge, combined with and tempered by life experiences!**

James was getting pulled back to previous experiences where he remembered and realized from his study of the Gnostic text of Thomas, which stated, *Belief without understanding is of little value.* James also remembered when his teacher, Kriya Kundalini Yogi, Govindan Satchidanada always asked, *What is more valuable, intelligence or wisdom?* Yogi Govindan would always answer, *Of the two, wisdom is much more valuable because the wise man has the ability to solve problems and deal with situations, whereas the intelligent man only has stored a bunch of facts and facts do not solve problems, in and of themselves! Much better is the life experiences one gains traveling through their lifetime!*

James continued, openly verbalizing the memories that chattered in his head, "Many people seem to believe being birthed into Earth through a Uterus/Vagina has inherent limitations as to how long we can live! But, does it really have to be that way? Yes, it is very possible the Anunaki manipulated our DNA to give us a short shelf life, like the Nexus 5 replicants in the movie, *Blade Runner*. It is clear from Sitchin's books that the ET Anunaki, who came here hundreds of thousands of years ago, pretty much manipulated the people of Earth to suit their purposes. And one of those purposes was to have compliant workers with short life spans so they would never reach a state of even quasi enlightenment! This was beneficial for the Anunaki, since they had generally compliant laborers, yet disadvantageous for us who just schlepped along, doing menial tasks!

Questions ran rampant in his mind. *Is there some inherent reason for this short "shelf life" in the DNA, or more just a generally accepted constraint on immortality of our existing bodies, rarely if even contested, as to the validity of these limitations? It is virtually universally believed by all people our deterioration and death are inevitable! Are there epigenetic factors (ways to change and modify our genes/RNA/DNA)?*

Stopping for a moment to quiet his racing mind, James then considered, "I know Dr. Newton and I covered some of the epigenetic factors in our book, *A Map to Healing and Your Essential Divinity Through Theta Consciousness*", wherein we discussed how certain types of meditations, including Kriya Kundalini Pranayam and the Tai Chi "Standing Meditation" could and would change our brainwaves to Theta level, and cause us to enter a more enlightened state of consciousness with a resulting lengthening of the telomere strands at the end of our DNA!. We also discussed how Sanskrit mantras like "The Gayatri Mantra" and the Mahamrityonjaya Mantra" would cause a **deeper level of consciousness and even effectuate healing in people!**

There is also another factor in regard to being birthed through a vagina/vaginal vortex or in another manner, James considered, I remember in William Henry's, *The Secrets of Sion*, there was a discussion of Gnostic texts which indicated Yeshua (Jesus) came to Earth from another planet in a Merkabah, otherwise known as a body of light, to serve humanity! The fact that most paintings of Jesus show an aura, a band of light above his head, indicates a confirmation of the Merkabah or body of light/Prana/Chi/God-life force! This Merkabah would be also verified by the so-called resurrection of Jesus because that which manifests itself as light, intense Prana/Chi/God-life force, cannot be extinguished! And as this light becomes more apparent around a human body, the higher the dimensions of consciousness, which can then be accessed and maintained! These higher dimensions manifest bodies more comprised of light and less the illusion of matter!

As James played with his thoughts, he mulled them over in his mind, and ultimately asked himself, How do you come to terms with the reality that whether you are "born" in a galactic vortex or a vaginal vortex, it should not make that much difference, in the end? Remaining in our current body in a state of immortality is far more important so the Elders can share their knowledge and wisdom to help make the needed changes to Planet Earth to bring it into a state of *Aleph Kaf Aleph*...a state of inherent perfection!"

Back to his internal contemplations, James thought, *this is what I am doing now and will do into the foreseeable future! Service to humanity is the game and in humility I will remain! In Hinduism we call this Bhakti and Jnana, yoga as a type of selfless devotion, but in the end, it is helping to uplift our fellow man/woman and not necessarily in that order! This is an important and crucial thing to remember, ha-ha! Here we go again with my state of Divine laughing! I wonder how my laugh sounds in a rabbit hole?*

CHAPTER TWO

Down the Rabbit Hole(s) and Then Some
What About Those "Silly Wabbits?"

––––––– ❦ –––––––

AS JAMES CONTEMPLATED the monumental task facing him, his mind would not let him rest... his thoughts flowed freely and he wondered, *Have I have bitten off more than I can chew? This is really a lot to "eat" and I do not want to be eating any "silly, widdle Wabbits!* Certainly James had seen enough people "bite the dust" lately; including his beloved wife, Ann, his mother and father, many friends from high school such as his friend Pedro, as well as several in-laws. *What was I thinking? I might really have to be crazy to even remotely consider this immortality gig! What are the odds for me pulling this off? For sure, accomplishing this would pay off big because of the astronomical odds involved!*

Shifting from thoughts to words, James spoke aloud, "Fortunately for me, I am crazy or worse, hahahaha! I think you have to be so to manifest what is believed impossible. Yet, *Vav Vav Lamed,* the 43rd Name of God from *The 72 Names of God* from "Exodus" in *The Torah,* tells me **the impossible is possible!"** Again, speaking aloud to no one, James once more vocalized his thoughts, "Once you have studied and repeated these names, like I have, you know their power by the miracles that are created in your life, as per the 3rd Name of God, Samesh Yod Tet!"

"Beyond even this, I have the strongest intuition: we have been bamboozled into believing death is inevitable and immortality is nothing more than a "remote theory! Remote and widely believed as an operational fact, but nonetheless without scientific merit and only verified by mispercepted religious dogma and actual editing of and outright discarding of religious texts!"

As this transpired, James' soul mate and deceased wife, Ann, was "checking in" from the lofty realms of High Heaven, and tuning into James' antics and thought processes! James turned his eyes upward and just smiled at his self-assessment. Ann was amused at the continually unique ways on the path of the left, which James repeatedly followed, being very left handed yet ambidextrous as well. Ann loved James' effusive humor and laughter, which had always served him well in tough situations and this would certainly be the most difficult task of all, at least perceptually, but something which he would effusively embrace, irrespective of the difficulty involved!

More deeply considering the specifics about people on Earth entering a state of an immortalized body, James realized Paramahansa Yogananda, Kriya Kundalini Yoga Avatar, who founded the Self Realization Fellowship, and Mary Baker Eddy, devout student of the old and new testaments of *The Bible* and author of *Science and Health with Key to the Scriptures,* never completely transfigured into a complete state of true immortality of the body. However, for sure and verified, neither of their bodies deteriorated for nine months after they left them behind, which in James' mind tread on the edge of immortality of the body, and left it in a state of soul disconnection, wherein the soul no longer inhabits the body and/or has taken a temporary leave, there from!

James felt confident their bodies were in a state of suspended animation and sustained by the Pranic energy within a breathless state of being, known as Soruba Samadhi, in Kriya Kundalini Yoga. Of course, said Samadhi is so deeply hidden in Indian texts *The Bhagavad Gita* and Kriya Kundalini Yogi Sat guru Patanjali's, *The Yoga Sutras,* as to be virtually unknown in not only Western civilization but in the Indian civilization as well.

However, James was also acutely aware that in the Kriya Kundalini Yoga tradition, popularized in Paramahansa Yogananda's *Autobiography of a Yogi,* there are many records of Satgurus, who are felt by many to be extremely evolved beings or the "true guru," going into a state of Soruba Samadhi, a permanent near death experience (NDE) where the Satgurus took their bodies into a state of immortality and also have the ability to transport themselves instantly, intra-and inter-dimensionally, to wherever they wish to be located.

James thought long and hard about how his beliefs were more than just folklore since the Sat gurus regularly make an appearance at the Kumba Mehla ecumenical religious gathering in India... mass pilgrimages of faith, Hindus, Yogis, and Sadhus, gather to bathe in a sacred river, chant Sanskrit praises to God and immerse themselves in a big celebration to Shiva/God. *How can the world not be aware; it is supposedly the largest peaceful gathering in the world where around 100 million were expected to visit in 2013?* Consoling him self with what he believed to be true, James tapped into the knowing power that essentially the Satgurus are sustained entirely by Prana (Chi, God/life force), as opposed to eating and breathing, and although there is no inherent need to do so, they may partake of food and drink on occasion.

According to all James had learned, these experiences occurred as far back as hundreds of thousands of years ago, possibly even more—to the time of about two millennia ago, as described in *Beyond the Mists of Time: When Trees Ruled the Earth* and yet the gravity and importance of these things fascinated James because this immortality gig had been pulled off already, and many times. Yet in India where it happened, only a handful of people knew about it and the occurrence was virtually unknown among the populace at large! The Sat gurus who achieved a state of overcoming death include: Agastyar, Boganathur, Thirumoolar, Rema Devar, Siddha Konkanavar, Valmiki, Babaji Nagaraj, and Mataji, among others lesser known. His mind was never willing to let him rest; James further pondered, *Does the fact this happened long ago, make these accomplishments irrelevant?* For him, it made things even more relevant since each person who does something makes it easier for each successive person to accomplish the same feat, without even big feet being necessary to "pull this off," as it were!

The idea of this "push" and "support" from the previous actions and thoughts of other people preceding us was something

James often contemplated. In fact the work of African biologist Lyall Watson, in *Lifetide,* revealed that Japanese Monkeys who washed their food had their actions later copied by other Monkeys who never even saw them wash the food. Ken Keyes also talked about all the implications of this in *The Hundredth Monkey.*

As farfetched as the idea of sustaining your body with Prana and the Sun, known as breatharianism or fasting might seem to others, James was fully aware the process is a basic inflow of electromagnetic energy into the body, nourishing it without the consumption of food. This is accomplished by breathing the electromagnetic energies of Prana/Chi/God-life force into the human body and holding the breath in the body for an extended period of time, staring at the Sun at sunrise and sunset and at a very advanced level, and bringing said energies into the body with no breathing at all but rather through magnetic attraction.

He also had confirmation of the feasibility of this practice from the documentary, *In the Beginning There was Light,* by Peter Arthur Straubinger. This documentary was completed using two subjects secured in a medical setting, where all kinds of medical instrumentation was used to measure what happened inside the body as closed circuit cameras ran 24/7 for the span of two weeks. Not only did the participants remain in vibrant health, they did not become emaciated or lose any muscle mass or body fat. They were never seen eating, urinating or defeating. One of the participants had not eaten food for seventy years—since the age of seven, which was substantiated by people who knew the man. "Is this amazing? Is this fortuitous? Undeniably, for me, it is, indeed!" James exclaimed effusively.

Additionally, James had seen an article from *The Journal of Metabolic Sciences* that indicated, "at least twenty five percent of what nourishes the body comes from some source other than food." James seriously contemplated whether he could prove the body could or would be completely sustained by Prana/Chi, since it seemed the amount of energy derived from food might well exceed the energy/Prana need to digest and assimilate the food! As James envisioned this he thought, *The bigger issue here is whether anyone other than me would be able to partially "digest" these concepts, let alone be able to completely comprehend such!* James knew the concept was contrary to everything believed in the field of nutrition and metabolism other than the article in *"The Journal of Metabolic Sciences.* "Hahahaha," the laughter ripped from James as he shouted, "I could really care less! When you go into "new territory," such are the perils one must face. And speaking of faces, I do in fact feel the presence of Ann nearby!

Then James recalled, "I seem to remember an article in *Reiki News*, put out by The International Study of Reiki Healing Center, where people's energy fields were measured by magnetometers." James knew of these devices, which measure magnetic and electrical energy fields, and show how significant amounts of energy emanated from many participants in a quantifiable study. He understood especially in the case of people in deep meditation and martial artists, huge amounts of energy were measured radiating from their bodies and hands, primarily because they learn how to attract and magnify huge amounts of Prana/Chi/Qui/God/life-force! This manifests an aura around the body, most concentrated in the

head and hands! It brought to his mind one of the amazing Alex Gray pictures that depicts the actual energy fields surrounding the human body. With the image burning in his mind, James thought, *this still does not prove the body can live on Prana alone and actually sustain a body instead of food! It certainly is, however, more pieces of evidence which indicate the body does have significant amounts of life sustaining electromagnetism associated with it and any practice or discipline which attracts and amplifies these things, I would need to pursue and actually* 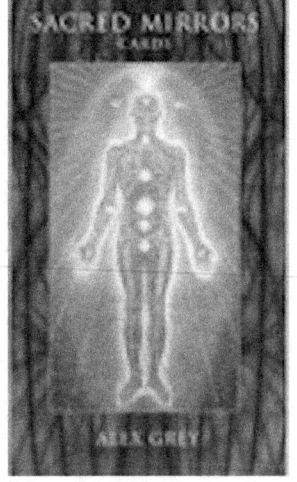 *have, to wit!* His thoughts took on more force as his they became loudly voiced questions, "Is this because of "Divine Guidance" or just a chance occurrence? More likely the former but who would eschew the later, if the result is the same?"

His mind was running on overtime, and he also remembered reading in *The Bhagavad Gita,* in the Kriya Yogi Paramahansa Yogananda translation (on page 369) where it was revealed something called the "Intelligent Cosmic Vibration" has two components, comprised of cosmic light, Yagna (fire), which also inherently includes Agna (light) and "Aum" (Amen/Holy Ghost), which is the primordial sound from whence emanates all creation. For James, the book further revealed on this page the "Cosmic forces" just described, are *"... the immediate source of all life and life sustaining food."* All this is contained in this Holy Scripture, from more than five thousand years ago in India. As James pondered this he realized, "these light and fire factors do nutrify the human body!" He also knew, just as important as the Agna and Yagna, the light and fire, would be the intense vibrational/cymatic properties of the vowel sounds in the Indian Sanskrit language contained in the sound of "Aum" and the powerful Sanskrit mantras, the *Gayatri Mantra* and the *Mahamrityonjaya Mantra.* Once again voicing his thoughts, James said, "The self evident part of this, for me, is the Vibration part of the Intelligent Cosmic Vibration. Things just keep stacking up and providing us a means to immortalize our bodies and not just as some "remote theory"!

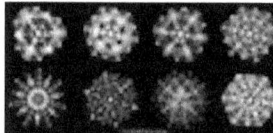 James' envisioned the geometric forms created on the atomic level, by the primordial sound, Aum/Om, which reminded him of the immense power of a one-syllable Sanskrit Mantra.

"Oh, my God," James said. "Dr. Newton and I included this information this in our book, *A Map to Healing and Your Essential Divinity Through Theta Consciousness.* It was in Chapter Eleven, and yet until now I failed to see the bigger significance of the concept. This literally says Prana/Chi/ God-life force is what nutrifies the body and not food per se, exactly as I have been claiming for a long time. The thought raced through his mind... *I feel like a dumb ass for missing the magnificence of this and the implications thereof but I must negate my denigration of myself by saying cancel, cancel.* James, with some frequency, used the Silva Mind Control's method of saying "cancel, cancel" to negate things you do not want going into your subconscious/ unconscious mind and manifesting in your life that negatively affecting you. *Awrggg, thought James! Sometimes when things are in front of our face we cannot even perceive them because we are looking too far into the horizon and we completely miss what is near to us! But I am not missing these things now which are directly related to the Kriya Kundalini Yoga I practice daily.* As though on cue, James remembered the mention of Dhyana and Samadhi, which were direct components of his specific yogic discipline, compounded by the supreme importance of the Sanskrit Mantras.

James continued this thread of thinking, *At the very worst, it is the Intelligent Cosmic Vibration's Force in the food that gives it the power to nutrify our bodies. Why, at the very best, can't only **this** force be necessary to sustain the human body since it can be breathed into the body without the transportation factor of food!* Laughing, James asked aloud, "Is it mere coincidence this breathing factor has long been specifically contained in the practice of Kriya Kundalini Pranayam? Go figure!"

James knew it is the ability to hold each breath inside the body for a long duration, which magnifies the Intelligent Cosmic Design /Prana/Chi/God/life-force, and provides the nourishment of the body, which is just not possible by inhaling and exhaling in a quick, shallow breath.

His awareness heightened, James deliberated, *Such shallow breathing does not allow for much permeation the above forces throughout the body!* He remembered reading several books regarding Taoist Breathing Canons—by writers such as Stephan T. Chiang, Steven Chaio and those of Mantak Chia—and recalled how the longer each breath remains in the body the more it is nourished with Chi! One concept in particular brought renewed visions to his mind as James thought, *I also remember the writers discussing how the animals like whales and giant sea turtles live extremely long lives because of their three to four minute per breathing cycle and how animals like dogs, who have a very short breathing cycle akin to panting, have very short lives.*

"Anyway, life is a continual process of learning and I feel very strongly at my core the Creator itself is in a process of continual learning. Many people have given me those "looneysville" eyes when I talk about this, but when I consider how we are inextricably linked to God via the Intelligent Cosmic Vibration, just maybe I am not so "looneysville" after all. He laughed and continued his diatribe with himself. "Hahahaha! And even if I am, I still laugh at this and feel laughing might be as big of a component in the search for immortality as all of the other things esoteric and scientific. After all, a laughing person is well known to be a healthy person with long telomere strands at the end of their DNA! And I know long telomere strands lead to radiant health and long lives and immortality!" Laughter had long been James' best friend and as his body shuddered with its energy, he further noted, "This is scientific reality, my friend, as opposed to random babble, and it is just TFT for those who do not like this!

James' thoughts were all over the place, and he thought of David Armstrong, who had a near death experience (NDE) and wrote the book, *Messages From the Spirit World*. Armstrong shared James' belief that humor and laughter are an inextricable part of living on Planet Earth. James asked himself, "Was it Armstrong who noted, "Pretty much, those who aren't laughing aren't living with much joy, 'boy oh boy?'" His mental perspective shifted to one of almost dying and then coming back to Earth and how it radically changes people's perspective about everything on Earth, as what transpired with David Armstrong! *It probably gives a person an inherent understanding of the 1st and 49th Names of God, which mean to create happiness! Did I mention happiness? Is there happiness therein?*

Well-read, James had more than a modicum of knowledge about the NDE experience. He had learned it not only shows death can be overcome, but healing even without surgical intervention as in the case of Marcos Berrios, who was known to not only came back into his body after being badly burned with third degree burns but healed of them with no skin grafts or surgery. His whole face was burned, yet it now looks normal! In this particular case, it was Marcos' determination he did not need surgical intervention that allowed him to pull this off!

James added to his thoughts a recount of David Roscher's severe spinal injuries from a bicycle accident, following which he refused the medical-surgical advice to repair spinal fractures and breakages and completely healed himself—in a matter of weeks—in place of the medical diagnosis he would never walk again without surgery and maybe even with it. By refusing to believe the prognosis and taking himself into a theta level mode of personal healing, David was able not only to walk, but run again as well!

Seconds turned into something much longer as James had an almost instant recall of the Facebook account David had posted of his experience:

> *It was Sunny that day, April 10 2013 and I thought it was great for a bike ride down hill to accomplish an errand. After my brakes got warmed up from use then wet from the rain the night before, my rim caliper rear brakes failed... Just as my speed exceeded 30 mph and only a 1/3rd the way down the hill on lower Mauna Kea. I began carefully using both front and rear brakes then was catapulted off the mountain bicycle...*

> *Nearly 8 hours later I was found, while it was still light out. I heard a Truck approach, heard my friend Pedro exit then speaking on his #Smart #Phone said to my mentor (Dr Robert Cassar) David Looks #Dead; then I spoke out, "I'm Not Dead yet!" and he was #Shocked! Four days later after Air #Ambulance flight #Surgeons urged me for five days to have #Surgery and I repeatedly #Refused! They said I would be Paralyzed and that I was #delusional and I mirrored the statement to them, "You're #Delusional!" I said, "You don't know what you're saying, and are guessing and have No Clue... I will #Overcome and #HEAL and have a #Total #recovery!" They were stunned. Gosh, I just #Love to #Run now! It's so #Liberating!*

As the pieces of the puzzle came together, James recognized an evolving picture... one that would continue to become more complete and clarified as the esoteric and scientific components integrated into James' search for immortality. James thought, *This whole quest gets more interesting every minute, every hour and*

17

every day. Maybe I can get some other crazies/followers who will follow their guru down one of life's "rabbit holes. He laughed out loud, but continued to process ideas of his quest, *I would promise not to ask them to drink any of the "Jonestown Kool-Aid or to eat any rabbits, as well!* Laughter trickled from his lips as he thought, *Maybe I can bamboozle Ann into helping me with this!*

"For sure, we are seeing the agenic factors of our thoughts and our emotions, which determine what and how we experience things and events in our lives!" James was aware this had already been ascertained in a clinical environment, regarding addictions issues, by Dr. Gabor Mate. The good doctor uncovered the real reason for various addiction issues as quite simply being afflicted by extreme pain. If this is the case, James, thought, *To deal with the pain, people use addictive substances. So to get out of pain, we need to receive love and assurance from some sources or sources! In the end, this must also be applicable to whether we live forever or deteriorate into a state of death! We must learn and know that our Creator/God loves us with such an unconditional intensity so as to know we are deserving of having an immortal body and we never were unworthy sinners nor every capable of being such!*

Words followed thought as James considered, "For sure, that will go over like a "lead turd" in the Christian Orthodoxy, but I have never let there myopic view of things limit my own perception and knowledge!"

"We also have the examples of many enlightened beings who have gone before us! So as well as the Kriya Kundalini Yoga Satgurus; Krishna and Rama, sons of God in India; and son of God, Yeshua/Jesus, let us not forget Thoth, also known as Hermes/Enoch/Quetzalcoatl, or Horus and Osirus, a god of death and rebirth, among others in Egypt, who attained an exalted state of immortality following *The Egyptian Book of the Dead* and working with the mind and body transforming energies in Lotus Consciousness. James knew and deeply understood this wisdom; it was revealed in the book, *Beyond the Mists of Time: When Trees Ruled the Earth,* and he felt confident the pyramids in Egypt were an accelerating factor into expanded consciousness and immortality

He also recalled the intense electromagnetic energies of the pyramids, which is chronicled in *The Giza Power Plant*, by Christopher Dodd, and James' co-authoring with Dr. Newton in *Pathways to God: Experiencing the Energies of the Living God in Your Everyday Life*. Each discussed the energies found inside and around the pyramids, and put the brain/mind in a state of expanded consciousness to see through the need for food and drink and even breathing as a means of sustaining the body in an incorruptible state being nourished by God-life force/ Prana/Chi. According to this collective of authors, the life force energies inside and around the pyramids had been measured and there were most definitely significantly higher energy fields measured—as opposed to the areas more distant from the pyramids.

James' mind immediately picked up the imagery of an energy field at the top of pyramids, which look similar to our own binary-pairs DNA, and the spiral that it part thereof. *At the very least*, he thought, *it is an intense Torus energy field, which* 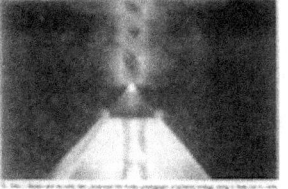 *affects anything inside it or and near its exterior*

No longer able to contain his thoughts, James felt both his questions and the coincident responses flow seamlessly from his mouth, "How do we measure the effects of the pyramid energies? Well this is easy! When we realize putting razor blades under pyramids will make them sharper and putting seeds under a pyramid will make them germinate faster and better! What would happen if a person regularly put their body under a pyramid form?

For James, in the past this line of questioning had led to deeper meditation experiences, increased sexual energy and pleasure and vastly enhanced psychic abilities. Each was the result of his experience in Samadhi, inside the Great Pyramid in Giza Egypt, where his breathing and heartbeat had ceased; a "flat line" of sorts. His memory did not fail and James assumed, *All of this was the result of brainwaves being shifted into to deep alpha and theta level and even upper delta. I am confident there is also an Intelligent Cosmic Vibration factor to all of this—as previously noted by the light that can be seen above and around a pyramid form. The intelligent result of this; being able to immortalize our bodies in the here and now!*

It was a rather sad state of affairs James had no audience; his delivery was articulate as he spoke aloud... to himself. "In his incarnation as Thoth in Egypt, the God of the moon, magic and writing, would certainly have had the availability of pyramids to magnify his Intelligent Cosmic Vibration and transport himself in the known state of immortality he is known to have achieved! Even more amazing is the fact that Thoth spent long life spans in Atlantis and Sumer, as Hermes Trismegistus in Greece, as Enoch in Palestine, and Quetzalcoatl in Mesoamérica. This somewhat immortalized Avatar also seemed to have teleported himself back and forth to some of the civilizations he concurrently inhabited! Such are the benefits and abilities of those who immortalize their body, which then becomes a vehicle, as per a Merkabah, allowing teleportation to any destination, with little effort beyond thinking and concentrating on a destination!

Speaking aloud apparently inspired James, for he continued his diatribe, "There is high validity and usefulness to Thoth's multi-disciplinary approach both to spiritual understanding and immortality. By combining *The Egyptian Book of the Dead, The Emerald Tablets of Hermes Trismegustis* (AKA *The Smagardine Tablets, The Kabbalah, The 72 Names of God* from *Exodus* in *The Torah* and *The Popol Vuh,* which just happens to be the only surviving Mayan esoteric text, among others.

Continuing, James said, "Now, if I were to use a multi-disciplinary approach, as just discussed, and used Kriya Kundalini Yoga and especially Kriya Kundalini Pranayam, as delineated in Patanjali's *The Yoga Sutras and* combined it all with the Indian Sanskrit mantras of *Om/Aum, The Gayatri Mantra* and *The Mahamrityonjaya Mantra...* something tells me I would have the best of all esoteric knowledge which would guide me to my destination of immortality!"

Questions plummeted his mind again and James silently queried, *How can I be so sure of that? Is it the signposts along the journey of my practices that bring this certainty of knowingness? Truly, even individually, these things have changed me in so many ways for the better; I never could have anticipated how much my understanding of things would be altered. What will happen when all of these things are combined? Is it possible; does it actually make immortalizing my body within the realm of the doable?*

Once more vocal in his assertions, and speaking to his invisible crowd, James carried on, "Oh! And for good measure, I should include Dr. J.J. Hurtak's *The Keys of Enoch* and *The Tibetan Book of the Dead,* also known as *Bardo Thodol,* which deals with what to do when you are in a state of transitioning to death and the rebirth that follows. But I am sure Ann, my recently deceased wife, can tell me as much about this as the *Bardo Thodol,* and since I am far more interested in remaining in my own body without death... this is not really fertile ground in my quest for immortality, or so it would seem!

"I have studied and contemplated Dr. Hurtak's book for more than three decades! Amazingly enough and coincidentally, *The Keys of Enoch* discusses the energy aspects of our bodies and how to create a Merkabah, or body of light. So right away, it is clearly evident there is an overlap with *Bhagavad Gita* and the Intelligent Cosmic Vibration and *The Keys of Enoch.* What a varied stew I am assembling!" Laughter rippled in the room as James laughed and said, "It seems I will be taking my approach to cooking, "the mélange" to my "immortality kitchen"! Even Don Quixote could not pull that off, ha!

"Of course, I will be learning many things from other sources along the way so I will be learning as I experience. Yet look at what I have learned and assimilated so far. The blessing of being led to this information is quite amazing. Certainly my beloved Ann was so very instrumental in all of this, giving me cutting edge information and insights into things!

"With this, I—and more importantly, we—will be given the opportunity to live the extended life times as Elders on Earth so we can create the New Heaven on Earth and follow the behest of the Godhead in *The Bhagavad Gita*! I can think of no better or worthwhile reason to do this immortality gig on Earth than restoring things to their perfect state, as per *Aleph Kaf Aleph*, the seventh Name of God from *The 72 Names of God*! So **let it be so!**

CHAPTER THREE

How to Be Free of a Deteriorating Body;
A Lot to Consider and a Lot to Apply so I
Can Take Flight Without Eating a Bite!

THERE WERE SOME ancillary issues that kept recurring in the immortality matter and they tugged at James' mind. Some people, to whom he was exposed, literally felt they could "fly" via the use of hallucinogenic substances. One such person, Dr. Terrence McKenna, was convinced using Psilocybin Mushrooms, Ayahuasca and other hallucinogens brought mind-altering insights into "the nature of creation and existence." Certainly, he uncovered many amazing things such as the fractal patterns in the *I Ching*, a revered Chinese system of divination (a way to uncover answers to things not self evident). Dr. McKenna has written many books about his experiences and insights including *True Hallucinations, The Invisible Landscape* and *Food of the Gods*. Unfortunately, Dr. McKenna died of brain cancer, despite his many insights into the "nature of consciousness" and shamanism. Certainly his insights into consciousness aid us in understanding the complexities of the nature of reality!

Other people like James' friend, Dr. Juan Acosta, an expert in brain tomography (mapping the brainwaves in a person's brain), thought Ayahuasca did the same thing or more than psilocybin. Dr. Acosta had taken more than three hundred "trips" on Ayahuasca and had relayed to James many of his experiences, which were altered states of consciousness that were very vivid, yet still not exactly what James was searching for..

Even one of James' students, David Roscher, relayed to James he went into Samadhi, the breathless state of living in a near death experience (NDE) when he took a DMT trip. However, when James started looking through studies on Ayahuasca and DMT, the active ingredient in Ayahuasca, he discovered that most people really were not in the breathless state of Samadhi but rather had the hallucination or simulation thereof.

And yet there would be critics who would say all of James' ideas about living in a state of immortality were just a big hallucinatory joke! And who could say with a certainty that a hallucination is not more than an illusion and rather another higher or parallel dimension? James found these perspectives very interesting and if life had taught James anything, it was to stay open minded so as to be able to learn and assimilate new information and perspectives as they came into his life!

A good example of this is when James read Dr. Jeremy Narby's book, *The Cosmic Serpent*. He got even more insight into Ayahuasca and he learned there were different brews of Ayahuasca, which depended whether Brugmansia, which is a genus of seven species of flowering plants in the family Solanaceae—or other plants were added to the mix! What James learned about the Amazonian Indians who used this substance was they decoded the DNA sequence more than two centuries before modern genetic researchers had done so.

The information catalyzed James to additional quiet contemplation, *this is impressive in and of itself and just as impressive is how these so-called primitive Indians could learn how to heal a patient and ascertain which herbs and foods to use by going into an Ayahuasca induced trance and the altered brainwaves in the theta and delta range that are accessed in the Ayahuasca trance consciousness! I know these are considered highly altered states of consciousness with a direct connection to the Creator and levels of great creativity, high performances and problem solving. And as it was chronicled, I can understand how these Indians seemed on the verge of entering into a state of immortality since there was some confirmation by other Indians, many of whom were centurions and more. It was said these centurions looked like they were forty or fifty years old. In thinking about it, I hold great respect for these Ayahuasceros, but maybe not so much for the recreational users of Ayahuasca, because of a difference in dedication and purpose.*

Closing his eyes and leaning back, James continued with his quiet deliberation, *somehow I can see Dr. Acosta has been vastly changed by his sojourns and experiences into the altered consciousness of Ayahuasca. I wish I could find out if the Indians engaged in any type of deep meditation in a non-Ayahuasca induced consciousness. I have not seen any indications of this and yet being in the altered brainwaves is the meditative state—just using another means to access something other than traditional meditation techniques. The fact these Indians decoded the DNA sequence and can effectuate healings of all types of maladies, established credibility for their work and achievements!*

Something nudged at James to voice his thoughts, and Ann heard him break the silence, "I am trying to find out what can be attributed to the Ayahuasceros' extended life spans. Is it because they are having genuine NDE's or just the pseudo experience thereof? Are they experiencing the Intelligent Cosmic Vibration in a manner described in *The Bhagavad Gita*? What I know for sure, Ann, is I respect what these Columbian Amazonian Indians have done! Yet at this point in time there is little for me to follow as it relates to immortalizing the human body, or is there?"

"I know what Yogi Govindan Satchidananda taught me about Kriya Kundalini Yoga is enough for me to build my Intelligent Cosmic Vibration through bringing the Yagna and Agna (fire and light) into my body through Kriya Kundalini Pranayam (a.k.a. Pranayama) breathing meditation as discussed in *The Bhagavad Gita* and *The Yoga Sutras*, by Kriya Yoga Satguru Patanjali and *Tirumandiram* by Kriya Yoga Satguru, Thirumoolar! The extended breathing cadence in Kriya Kundalini Pranayam is unlike any other processes to which I have been exposed and this does not exist in Kundalini Yoga or Taoist Breathing Cannons or Qui Gong. Undeniably, the Indian Sanskrit Mantras are an integral part of kick starting the Intelligent Cosmic Vibration! These things just always work in expected and unexpected ways to expand my consciousness and understanding of things—especially deep esoteric matters!

"God, Ann, I will never forget when Govindan was teaching me Pranayam in level one Kriya Kundalini Yoga... I flat lined, going into the NDE state of Samadhi and a concurrent Kundalini Awakening. It is almost impossible to describe the euphoric feelings, of being able to exist without breathing and the tremendous energy surge of the awakening and being immersed in an intense energy field of God; it was intensely sublime!

"I know combining the Sanskrit Mantras, including *Aum, The Gayatri Mantra* and *The Mahamrityonjaya Mantra,* which are part of The Intelligent Cosmic Vibration will create the effects and ensuing miracles discussed in *The Bhagavad Gita.* This comes from the cymatic /vibrational power in the Sanskrit vowel in the words therein! I wonder what would happen if I joined the practice of Pranayam with the internal recitation of the Sanskrit Mantras concurrently; just what kind of magic/miracles might occur? Certainly, such a joining of these two things is not discussed in any Yogic or Hindu text I have been exposed unto! So therefore, being the fool I am, as per the fearless Fool of the Tarot, I certainly must begin to join those things together. Let the fun and results begin... ha-ha! And fun and results I will have as I reap the rewards of my efforts!

"The calming and energizing effects of the vowel sounds in the Sanskrit language with settle and balance the emotions of the most colicky baby or angry or depressed human! So when I combine the Pranayam with the Sanskrit Mantras I will only be benefitted and brought closer to my quest for immortality of the human body."

"In fact, in some sense, there really is no need for a quest, in at least two respects, since I have been created perfectly as per *Aleph Kaf Aleph*, the seventh Name of God and eternally, as per *Hey Resh Chet*, connected inextricably to the light, the 59th Name of God! Yet apparently my mind needs the discipline of going through a process so I can claim the immortality that is already mine! Weird that is but necessary it is, or so it would seem! *Se la vie, mon ami, oui?"*

"So what is going to happen combining practices that boost my Intelligent Cosmic Vibration with the understanding I am going to garner from studying and contemplating *The 72 Names of God* from Exodus in *The Torah* in Chapter Fourteen, Verses 19-21, as well as *The Emerald Tablets of Hermes Trismegustis, The Pattern on the Trestle Board,* by Dr. Paul Foster Case, and *The Keys of Enoch,* by Dr. Hurtak? The only impediment to my entering a state of Samadhi and the breathless state and Breathairianism, the process of living without food, is a lack of discipline, which provides the focus necessary to accomplish my goal! Certainly Ann has an invaluable perspective about this!"

James continued, as though he had an audience before him, who were puppets, hanging on his every word, "I wonder, however, how many people will leave their Cannabis/Marijuana, which is an easier way to enter the altered/higher realms of consciousness and go down this deeper path with me? When I bring up this subject with my Cannabis using friends, they openly agree with me what I found has a deep validity, underlying the nature of everything! However, I feel they have a resistance to actually practicing such in a disciplined manner, applying the protocols of Kriya Kundalini Yoga, including Kriya Dhyana structured meditations and Kriya Pranayam, the breathing meditation! That mood-enhancing endorphins are stimulated by Cannabis make it a hard substance from which to withdraw, and therefore does not seem to be incentive to do so!"

"Yet the amount of endorphins and health enhancing effects released doing Kriya Kundalini Pranayam and the Sanskrit mantras has been quantified so it is only a matter of having the discipline and patience to transition to something higher! The benefit of Yogic breathing, Sudarshan Kriya, which is similar to Pranayam, was quantified by Fahri Saatcioglu in a study at the University of Oslo, where it was discovered this deep breathing had an effect on a practitioner's genes that led to a lengthening of their telomere strands. I know this always leads to improved health and a longer life span, invariably! For me too... I feel the benefits of the deep breathing!"

"You can really get addicted to Pranayam, as I have, as long as you program your mind it has innumerably more benefits than the effort and discipline required doing this every day! In the early stages of you practice of Pranayam, there are these recurring doubts, which reside in the subconscious mind, as to whether there are real benefits to be reaped from practicing such! I am a testament to the fact that this is more than worthwhile, as my psychic abilities, sexual prowess, creative juices, problem solving and the ability to easily live in the fourth and fifth dimensions, as opposed to the third/turd dimension, are off the charts! Likewise, the amount of endorphins produced during Pranayam is rather staggering, so I am basically in a good mood all the time!

"Now, endorphin enhancing effects also occur with the inhalation of Tobacco, as well as Cannabis, and that is why it is so hard to stop smoking cigarettes and Cannabis, as well!. The Ayahuasceros, as discussed in Dr. Narby's book, *The Cosmic Serpent,* say Tobacco is a mild hallucinogen and can lead to altered states of consciousness. But with the regular use of Tobacco and Cannabis you have issues of Emphysema and Bronchial problems so is this really **not a zero sum game**... at least not in the quest for immortality. Of course you could vaporize your Cannabis and your Tobacco!

Then somewhat out of the blue, but not surprising to James, his recently deceased wife, Ann, established contact with him and chimed in, " You know, James, I so much agree with you about the Cannabis issue. I really wish it was illegal, I think it would truly be for the betterment of humanity!

James then replied, "Why, thank you so much for gracing me with your presence, Ann, as you have descended, in a manner of speaking, from the lofty perches of high heaven! I felt you lurking in the shadows, as it were! You know I do not really want to illegalize anything, but more want people to make their decisions based on contemplation and evaluation rather than laws that try to force them into acting in a certain manner. Essentially, these laws never really change people's behaviors, anyway, since people have used Cannabis for decades and even millennia! And the pathetic human beings, known as politicians, **never follow their own laws either and that as in never ever, to wit!**

Ann, sensing the increasing passion James felt, responded, "When you put things as you just did, I guess you are right but I simply do not see Cannabis beneficial overall. Anyway, I wanted to thank you for the novel you wrote about my life and I love the title, *An Angel Not Perceived*! You called me an angel from the time we first met and you portrayed such in the book!

James, happy to have his angel to share so many of the thoughts that were plummeting his conscious, exclaimed, "Well, you might not know this, Ann, but many people use Cannabis in place of anti-depressants and considering the terrible side effects of drugs like Ritalin and Prozac, which can make people extremely violent, among other very bad things, Cannabis would be a better choice for this. Of course, an even better way to deal with depression is to reprogram the mind of the person depressed. You remember how well that was covered in *A Map to Healing and Your Essential Divinity Through Theta Consciousness*. As for *An Angel Not Perceived*, it was the easiest book I ever wrote because I wanted to get your poignant story out there since you lived such a low key life where most people would not recognize your great academic and life experience achievements, in regard to Kriya Kundalini Yoga and Hinduism! I tried to minimize my presence in the book as much as possible and concentrate on you!

Humbled by the love and devotion James showered on her, Ann quietly replied, "There is a lot of validity to everything you said, but I really came to connect with you because I so much want you to pull off this quest of immortalizing your existing body so as to remain as an Elder and help create Heaven on Earth, as Mary Baker Eddy stated was possible in *Science and Health with Key to the Scripture* and as per *Aleph Kaf Aleph*, the seventh *Name of God* that restores things to their perfect state! Also remember, I previously told you to control your anger about things so as to not waste valuable Prana/Chi/God Life Force so your body can store enough energy to enter Soruba Samadhi, or that immortality you seek."

"Anyway, I've been keeping an eye on you, and recently realized that what causes your anger and frustration is the Prana getting blocked inside your body when you express frustrated emotions. So when a perceived negative situation arises in your life, simply view it without reaction and use deep diaphragmatic breathing to relax yourself and allow the energy to flow unblocked again! You might also have to remove some gunk or bad programming from your brain/computer/subconscious, as per your theta healing protocols in *A Map to Healing and Your Essential Divinity Through Theta Consciousness*. You are dealing with bio-memories from your past, on the subconscious or unconscious level and actually you are unaware of these things. My concern is how they keep fueling your anger, and I need you to know so you know how to undo this... so do such, please!"

Knowing she held James as a captive audience by now, Ann continued, "For sure, you should integrate *The 72 Names of God* from *Exodus* of *The Torah* since there are so many powerful things to consider, including the Theta Consciousness healing protocols you shared therein, which are very similar to a Christian Science Healing treatment. I know you resonate strongly with the seventh name of God, *Aleph Kaf Aleph*, and the perfection underlying all creation, *Aleph Lamed Daled*, which represents protecting ourselves from evil and other people's negative emotions and *Hey Aleph Aleph* that creates order from chaos and is directly associated with *Aleph Kaf Aleph*."

Trying her best to motivate James to less anger, Ann carried on, "I also know you like *Yod Chet Vav*, which removes obstacles, *Mem Nun Daled*, about overcoming fears, and *Resh Hey Ayin*, where we seek to find the good in the bad! Also, you and I used to talk about *Vav Vav Lamed*, which makes the 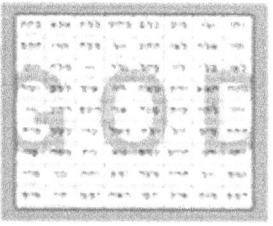 impossible possible, *Samesh Aleph Lamed*, which is the power of prosperity, and *Pey Vav Yod*, to use for dispelling anger, and *Mem Bet Hey*, which is putting thoughts into action."

As though she may never have another chance to remind James of all they had shared and learned, Ann enjoined James' vision with her own, as she delivered her truths, "And finally there is your other very favorite besides *Aleph Kaf Aleph* which is restoring things to their perfect state and *Hey Resh Chet*, connected to the Light/God, the Agna and the Yagna... the light and the fire! However, **in the end, everything distills down to *Hey Hey Ayin,* which is unconditional love** and I mean in everything and aspect of your life!

Feeling somewhat calmer, and wanting Ann to know he had hung on every word, James replied quickly, "I agree with you—and even more. The thing is, when I can teach these names in a class, people get pulled in and really getting excited about them. But if I just share some of the names of God in public, I see people's eyes glazing over and they kind of tune out! I think I see that more in people of orthodox religious views and less in people who are possessed or obsessed about knowing everything about God as is humanly possible and the personal transformation that comes from this! James closed his eyes and saw the imagery of the chart emblazoned on his mind.

Source: The 72 Names of God from Exodus 14: Verses 19-21 of the Torah.

"You know James," Ann responded, "Basically anything about everything is contained in these *72 Names of God* and I clearly remember how enthralled with each one you were when I shared them with you. And of course, you know Dr. Paul Foster Case used these names in his *Builders of the Adytum* lessons, each and every one! I know you are as astonished as I am these names have rarely been embraced by either Jews or Christians and yet they are the foundation, the very substrate of the entire *Torah* and *The Old Testament*. And then once you start studying these names of God you have a greater clarity about things and you start to get the feeling your immortality quest is not so looneysville, as you so often have termed it!"

James countered back with, "I could just say 'duh' and let it go at that, but I will elaborate as I tell you, correctamundo and then some, Ann. As heretical as this may seem, you could really dispose of the rest of *The Torah* and *The Bible* if you truly embraced *The 72*

Names of God! In fact, we might actually be better off if this actually happened because this small part of *The Torah* is a concentrated version of things, whereas the rest of it seems to be the chronicling of the lives of the Anunaki ET's who were here and might still be here!"

"If only ten percent of the populace would study and embrace these names, in the vein of Ken Keyes', *The Hundredth Monkey*, it could easily catalyze the perfection of *Aleph Kaf Aleph*, or at the worst, get the ball rolling for the rest of the world! The vibrational power of the Hebrew vowels has the ability to change things and people, very quickly and powerfully! In short order, perfection would be ushered in, with the ensuing realization we do not have to grow old or die and with that, concomitantly, we could create the New Heaven on Earth. There is nothing wrong with growing chronologically old, but believing in this sense of "oldness" leads to eventual degeneration and death! Certainly, Dr. Ellen Langer's study on aging at Harvard University in 1979 gives powerful evidence of what I have just relayed to you."

James' energy shifted, and he found his thoughts wandering across the great plains of his fertile mind, *In this study, male subjects in their seventies were taken to a resort where they had no outside contact with the World and these men were subjected and surrounded with everything from the 1950's and 1960's, including what they ate, the books and magazines they read, the music they listened to, the TV shows and movies they watched, the furnishings they were surrounded with and the clothes they wore. After two weeks, every participant looked visibly younger including the removal of wrinkles, they felt better with more energy and less aches and pains, and had a more positive outlook on life than before the study.*

Speaking once again to Ann, as though she had to hear his thoughts, James spoke aloud, "So this is part of the immortality frontier, as it were, learning to control the mind and its ensuing perception and emotions, the agenic factors, and directing these things in a manner where we lengthen our telomere strands at the end of our DNA so that we can propel ourselves into immortalizing our existing bodies! In fact, Ann, I found this most amazing article in a newsletter called *Nautilus,* entitled, "How to Unlearn Disease."

"The article, written by post doctorate neuroscientist, Kelly Clancy, reveals how the **brain can learn to be sick! But, it can also learn how to unlearn a disease, pain, and emotional issues.** Clancy described an actual procedure where neurosurgeons cut a spinal nerve that was causing pain in the lower body of a patient. Yet after the surgery, despite the nerve no longer being connected to the pain area, the patient still felt severe pain. This is an example of how the body learns pain! And it is also reveals how the body learns to accept death as a natural and necessary process, which is inevitable for all human beings, sooner or later and sometimes, even sooner than later!

"Yet get this, Ann, neuroscientists have found by stimulating the vagus nerve and the brain, pain, disease and emotional trauma can be completely eliminated! This would take the Cannabis factor out of play; Marijuana would become redundant! And these scientists have discovered hypnosis, self-hypnosis, deep Yoga meditations and the Tibetan Buddhist meditation of Tummo, known as inner fire, can effectively eliminate pain, disease and emotional trauma, including PTSD! Even learning just how to relax, which all the above things do, has helped epileptics to eliminate the seizures they experience!

Ann replied in a most ebullient manner, "Good God, James! These are many of the things we have known for more than two or three decades. This confirmation of what we knew is so incredibly cool... cooler than liquid nitrogen, ha-ha!"

James then laughingly responded, "Well, I would never claim to be God, but all compliments I accept, ha-ha!! All of this can be done with a Christian Science healing treatment, Silva Mind Control, Neuro Linguistic Programming (NLP), hypnotherapy, EFT, Tapping, Theta Healing and Theta Consciousness Reprogramming as per *A Map to Healing and Your Essential Divinity Through Theta Consciousness,* which pretty much includes how all of these things work! And for sure, work they do! These things give us the power to take destructive and limiting programs our of our subconscious/unconscious minds/brain-computers!"

James continued, "So if these healing of pain and emotional issues can be achieved with the various things just mentioned, why can't immortality of our existing bodies be achieved using the same approaches just mentioned? The answer, from me, is there is no impediment to doing such!"

James' excitement grew exponentially as Ann then exclaimed, "Yes, duh, there are no cogent contra arguments which can be proffered to refute your question, which is more like an exclamation. By paying attention to the agenic factors of the emotions and thoughts, this is a revolutionary way to manifest that immortality you are so focused upon! Yet, we should also discuss *The Emerald Tablet of Hermes Trismegustis*, AKA *The Smagardine Tablet* because therein are the most amazing insights into the nature of creation and by inference, immortality of our bodies. And you and I both love the Dr. Paul Foster Case. For sure, the Dr. Case translation of *The Emerald Tablets* has such great clarity, even better than the Sir Isaac Newton version. In the beginning of this text, Hermes states, "...that which is above is that which is below and that which is below and that which is above for the performance of the miracles of the One Thing. And all things are from the One Thing, by the mediation of the One, so all things have their birth from this one thing by adaptation. This is the father of all perfection, or consummation of the whole world. Its power is integrating if it be turned into earth."

Knowing she had James held in rapt attention, Ann felt confident to continue, " I believe what we are told here is there is a non duality or a coherent field where the foundation of creation, at the atomic level, supports the above level which is human and galactic and beyond and vice versa! But for most people, it is easier to see how the atoms on the atomic level bleed up into a more complex level, including us and our Earth, our solar system and our galaxies! We are told there is this perfection on all levels of Creation, and they are inextricably inter-related!

James was quick to maintain, "I already agree with you and more! We already know Dr. Newton and I proved how this happens in *A Map to Healing and Your Essential Divinity Through Theta Consciousness* and we revealed an order and recurring perfection of geometric forms on the atomic level, as per Valery P. Kondratov's *Geometry of a Uniform Field*. So this really proves what Mary Baker Eddy was claiming in *Science and Health with Key to the Scriptures*, God created everything perfectly, irrespective of almost everyone believing otherwise! Just remember, Hermes is a personage of great knowledge and was venerated as Thoth in Egypt, Sumer and Atlantis, Hermes in Greece, Enoch in Palestine and Quetzalcoatl in Central America. And not only he had great knowledge but commensurate abilities also, including the ability to teleport himself intra-dimensionally and inter-dimensionally; he could move from one place to another at the speed of light, or close thereto!

"There is no doubt in my mind about what you have shared, James. Just remember Hermes also said, as closely as I can recall the words, 'Thou shalt separate the earth from the fire, the subtle from the gross, suavely, and with great ingenuity. It ascends from earth to heaven and descends again to earth, and receives the powers of the superiors and of the inferiors. So thou hast the power of the whole world, therefore let all obscurity flee before thee. This is the strong force of all forces, overcoming every subtle and penetrating every solid thing. So the world was created. Hence, were all wonderful adaptations of which this is the manner."

As their natural flow of shared intellect continued, James replied, "And... this also underlines what Mrs. Eddy was saying, which is there is no matter and everything was created by God, Spirit. Even Quantum Mechanics suggests the same thing, regardless of the search for dense matter at the Hadron Collider in Switzerland, an atomic collider where atoms are smashed in a search for the **elusive dense matter**. So if there is no deteriorating matter, and all your evidence indicates such, why look for it? **Why not look for energy?**"

"Well all of this is directly related to my quest for immortality of this existing body, Ann, and indicates than I am much less looneysville than some people have conjectured, ha-ha!

"You are enjoying your triumph here quite a bit aren't you James?

"Whatever would make you think like that, my angel?"

For some moments the banter carried the conversation in a light-hearted tone and Ann's intention to diminish the anger and frustration she had seen James experience, let her to shift back to the matter at hand. "Well you rather deserve some slight arrogance on this, ha-ha!! Actually, you are not arrogant at all, James, but rather feeling exonerated and validated in relation to the scorn you have experienced for all the negativity you receive when you talk about the real possibility of immortalizing our bodies!

"Yes, it is nice, and then some, to have the validation of something I have gone way out on a limb to promote! But I guess we should consider Dr. Paul Foster Case's *The Pattern on the Trestle Board*, while we are still in a state of faux arrogance, ha-ha! Really, this is a further explanation of *The Emerald Tablet* in a series of eleven declaratory sentences, some of which I will share."

All the power that ever was or will be is here now.

From the exhaustless riches of its Limitless Substance, I draw all thing needful, both spiritual and material.

I recognize the manifestation of the undeviating justice in all the circumstances of my life.

I look forward with confidence to the perfect realization of Eternal Splendor of Limitless Light.

In thought and word and deed, I rest my life, from day to day, upon the sure Foundation of Eternal Being.

The Kingdom of Spirit is embodied in my flesh.

"Well Mr. Smarty Pants," Ann chimed in, "Just remember I was the one who introduced you into these amazing declaratory statements about the nature of reality, formulated by the amazing Dr. Case. Each statement builds on the next and it is really possible for us to have all our needs met if we actually allow such into our lives. Too many times, subconscious programming in our minds creates serious roadblocks to this happening. And even more amazing is the concept of inherent state of justice, within which we can live our lives. Beyond even that, it is so cool how Dr. Case connects Limitless Light, which is Prana/Chi/God-life force, and our eternal being and our spiritual nature, which is the foundation of our immortality. So, Sir James of the Smarty Pants, the things you have been talking about and writing about in your books is validated here... and more."

"Well, Ann, I do not know if my pants are smart but I would like to believe I am, at least a wee bit! My pants think I am smart, too, but of course, they are a partial audience! Additionally, I remember when you shared these prescient statements from Dr. Case and how it blew my mind how insightful they are. Dr. Case's book, *Spiritual Alchemy* is probably "the book" on the subject of Alchemy in modern times. Certainly he shares a lot of things of how to transfigure the body into its essential elements of Light/Prana/Chi/God-life force using salt, mercury and water. These quixotic elements seem to have the power to stimulate the process of immortality! And yet Dr. Case practiced Kriya Kundalini Pranayama and I personally consider that has more power than all the protocols of Esoteric Alchemy!"

Thinking about The myriad properties of *The Pattern on the Trestle Board and* taking a moment to wrap his head around the previous conversations with Ann, James held to his internal thoughts as he looked out at the blue, clouded sky and wondered about Ann, and other things related to their previous exchange. *Obviously these properties are not much accepted within much of the general scientific community, yet the scientists within the discipline of Quantum Mechanics understand this as an inherent reality. And yet Dr. Case says the ultimate path to immortalizing the body cannot be completely explained and must be intuited and uncovered by the initiate on this quest! Unfortunately, for Dr. Case, as evolved as he was he did not manage to pull of the immortality gig during his last lifetime on Earth! Yet using Dr. Case's amazing knowledge one can never go wrong!*

"Say, Ann, maybe Case **could** have gone into a state of immortality, but just choose to leave planet Earth, like you did! I think Dr. Bruce Lipton's book, *The Biology of Belief,* has a lot of information germane to search for immortality."

"Do you think?

"Yes, I think so or a semblance thereof, Ann. The essential task here is to get our thoughts in alignment with concentrating on the positive and the perfect so we create perfection, as per *Aleph Kaf Aleph*, so we live in a state of perfection, devoid of bodily deterioration. Only then will we be actually living within the benefits of being energy/light, actual realized energy/light, which does not deteriorate or become debilitated!

CHAPTER FOUR

Using Belief, Altered Perceptions, Directed Energy and More to Get to the Core!

————— ⸻⸻ —————

DR. LIPTON'S BOOKS *have been most amazing*, thought James, *because they vastly transcend his training in biology*. A lot of times someone has an epiphany and is taken beyond one discipline where they have an expertise and start working within a cross disciplinary approach to things. *Hmmm, this is when amazing occurrences tend to happen, which applies to Dr. Lipton as well as other scientists and researchers!* After some consideration, James was confident this was exactly the approach James and Dr. Newton used in *A Map to Healing and Your Essential Divinity Through Theta Consciousness*!

As James pondered what Dr. Lipton was saying in *The Biology of Belief*, he reflected, *this certainly goes with the things I am finding that are germane to immortality! Lipton has found the research that proves we are not victims of our DNA and RNA/genes, nor are these things set for our entire lifetime and "set in concrete."*

Thoughts slowly formed themselves as words, and James commented, "Rather, he is revealing our DNA and cells are in a constant state of flux, where they are affected by our thoughts and the energy they are subjected unto! And this gives us liberation from a static DNA and ushers in the field of Epigenetics where we can reprogram DNA and reprogram it constantly, anyway, whether we know it or not!

Ann then chimed in, " Well, James, of the smartest pants, ha-ha, this fits right in with Kelly Clancy's *How to Unlearn Disease* and using positive thoughts, meditation and implants to affect our thoughts and eliminate sickness, pain and emotional trauma in our lives! Additionally, you have that article in *Scientific American* from December 4, 2012 by research scientist Robert Martone, from the Covenance Biomarker Center of Excellence in Greenfield, Indiana, where there is traceable evidence of a mother transferring her cells to the blood and the brain of her baby!

There was even evidence these cells can be transferred when the mother is nursing her baby, so imagine what would happen if the mother was in a state of joy and positivity, which we already know certainly affects our DNA and makes the telomere strands of the DNA longer and more vibrant. Could you entrain the baby into a state of immortality from the beginning of its life? Would that also circumvent sickness, disease and genetic defects in the baby? This is kind of one of those "duh" moments, at least for me!"

James responded, "Duh, is right! That is exactly what I was thinking too, so that makes two of us, as it were, ha! Both of these studies really can just as easily apply to immortality as much as to sickness, pain and emotional despair/PTSD, because it is the meditation and we control our emotions and thoughts, which ultimately determine how everything works out in the end! And of course you know Louise L. Hay, in her book, *You Can Heal Your Life*, talks extensively about the emotional and mental components of sickness, disease and mental disorders. So why would this not apply to life extension and immortalizing our current body? There is no reason I can conjure up to contradict this, even in the worst scenario!"

"And Ann, remember, there was an article published in *The Journal of Psychoneuroendocrinology*, from studies in Wisconsin, Spain and France, which noted where gene alterations could be detected in people in a concentrated state of meditation. These gene alterations had analgesic and anti-inflammatory effects on the human body. So just plain meditation will and does modify DNA! Imagine, Ann, what would happen if the subjects of the study performed the very deep level meditation of Kriya Kundalini

Pranayam! Now I know why I live basically pain free... because of the assiduous amounts of Kriya Kundalini Pranayam I perform daily!"

"Additionally," James continued, "we have the Samantha Project which gives us strong evidence that people who meditate intensely have telomere strands at the end of their DNA that are thirty percent longer than the control group in the study. The double benefit from this intensive meditation is enhanced brainwaves in the alpha-theta-delta range and the enhanced consciousness that ensues there from, and we also get improved health and extended life spans! Now, that, Ann, is completely coolsville. "

The next day James had the most exciting thing he had discovered in a long time to share with Ann. He had actually been looking for the scientific confirmation of something he had known intuitively for at least five years. Relaying this to Ann James shared, "Guess what I found Ann? I finally found some hard evidence from a study undertaken at Nithyananda Dhyanapeetam's International Headquarters in Bengaluru, India on the physical and mental transformation of the human body in regards to Pranayama and Kundalini Awakening! Comprehensively, it showed major alteration of negative physical conditions of the human body and mental/emotional conditions of the brain-mind that would indicate genetic and DNA alteration on a level unknown in the Western World and actually the entire world. So I am real damn happy and then some and some then!"

"Like duhsville," Ann laughingly exclaimed. "I can see and feel your elation. Your persistence has been rewarded and fittingly so, since both you and I spent so much time trying to scientifically validate what we intuitively knew! So kudos, and then some and some then, as you would say!"

"Do you know what else I discovered?" James continued. "We know there are two kinds of DNA and/or DNA functions! One is **structural** DNA and the other is a **language** DNA. So imagine what would happen if a mother repeated Sanskrit Mantras and *The 72 Names of God* in Hebrew in the baby's presence. The language/vibration of these would most likely have an ameliorating effect on its DNA, health, happiness and longevity! This really just blows my mind! Now how do I blow other people's minds?"

"And then there is the amazing Mary Baker Eddy and her book, *Science and Health with Key to the Scriptures,* which vastly predated Louise Hay's book, *You Can Heal Your Life.* Her work is an in-depth look about how our emotional and mental outlook affects our health, and this was more than a century and a half ago! It was the positivity Mrs. Eddy exuded in *Science and Health* that initially convinced me I did not have to suffer from disease and sickness, nor did I have to die, since as she revealed, 'Man is created in the image and likeness of God.' I am more than sure God is not dying so it would seem I do not have to, either, ha-ha, fafaha!"

Ann quietly took in all James had to say as he continued, "And laughter should be in the immortality equation also, Ann, and there are university studies which prove this. One study at Loma Linda University proved people who laugh not only have better memory retention of facts, it also proved, and this is really important, laughter created lower levels of cortisol in people, which means they are less stressed! And not to forget the study at the University of Maryland, which revealed people who laugh will have fewer coronary problems, including heart attacks! So we would much more than likely have gene and DNA alteration in this case as well!

Ann laughingly replied, "Well, James, your pants seem to be becoming even smarter the more you laugh and share. There must be a divine component to our laughing, putting us closer to our Creator/God, and allowing us to attract and bask in this Pranic field that emanates there from! And now, ha-ha, fafaha, I am even using your phraseology with my words! What next, will I sprout a beard? Anyway, James, your vibe is no jive, or at least that is what you have been claiming, ha-ha!!

James good-naturedly exclaimed in kind, "Jab and gab is certainly a gift you have, Ann! I guess you needed to descend from the realms of High Heaven to get some good laughing down here on Earth. Almost anything, in even the direst circumstances, has something funny and/or bizarre that can elicit laughter. And for *mua*, this is a key to living on Planet Earth, but even more if you are here for the immortality gig, as am I!" Feeling a bit sassy, James kept the banter going. "When the "shiite" hits the fan, repeating the 39th Name of God, *Resh Hey Ayin*, finding the good in the bad, will always pull you out of a funk and the gunk, and you will no longer smell or feel like a skunk! This can also be used to eliminate anger as well as the 56th Name of God, *Pey Vav Yod* and put us in the laughing mode. Laughing our way to immortality might be as farfetched as almost everyone would contend!"

"For sure. Of course, we know from several studies that tapping the Thymus gland will make people happier. This is a new finding but we have known, or at least a few people have, that tapping the Thymus gland also pumps up the immune system. So when you look at both of these things, they are both immortality factors, since happiness and health both lengthen the telomere strands at the end of our DNA and at the worst, allow us to live longer, if not forever, ha-ha! Some people are too lazy or challenged to learn how to use mediation, Sanskrit mantras, laughing and happiness to lengthen their telomere strands. For them, they can use "Product 'B'" created by Bill Andrews at Sierra Labs. Some people really are too lazy, but guess what? The 1st and 49th Name of God, *Vav Hey Vav*, which are one and the same thing, are about creating happiness by fixing our problems!"

"The fact this name is used twice in *the 72 Names of God*, is not just some chance reiteration! It would rather indicate a primal importance of this name. When you conjoin this with the 63rd Name of God, *Ayin Nun Vav*, which is "appreciation." It could be recognized it is more than likely creating happiness would lead to the emotion and thoughts of appreciation. And we know from many sources, including *Science and Health with Key to the Scriptures*, effusively extol the virtues of appreciation and the resulting benefits of prosperity that comes to us with such a mindset! So we might infer from this, being grateful for everything we have +received in our lives would prime the pump to manifesting an immortalized body! Is that stretching too far?"

Such an expanded topic led to more conversation, "Actually, it might be not stretch us enough and certainly laughing and happiness would be an integral part to engage in more of this, likewise! Part of Yoga is stretching, the Asanas, and the goal should be to stretch your body more each day you perform these stretches! So why not daily stretch the limits and bounds of our minds, likewise?"

"What I real find ironic and actually even stupefying is how the organizer of the an event I spoke at in Los Angeles had the temerity to tell me that my laughing on the panel discussions, in which I participated, was unprofessional and I should refrain from such. And then I was castigated for talking about orgasms and sexuality as a mean to spirituality and even immortality and I was censured on the panel from further discussion on the topics at hand. I will not say the organizer's name, as there is no need for public embarrassment of this person but you know whom I am talking about anyway!"

Ann spent some quiet moments in her own mind as she tried to sum things up, and finally exclaimed, "I do know what you are talking about and it is extremely ridiculous you would be pilloried for laughing and sharing your extensive knowledge of sexuality as very few people have. But we know from all you and I have discussed, James, our outlook on things determines what we experience in our lives and this is a "hard and fast" rule. So you and Dr. Newton developed your acclaimed "Theta Consciousness Reprogramming," as per your book *A Map to Healing and Your Essential Divinity Through Theta Consciousness and* Vianna Stibal has her "Theta Healing." Notwithstanding, there are also hypno-therapy/hypnosis, Neuro Linguistic Programming, EFT, and Silva Mind Control where we can re-program/redirect the programs in our subconscious/unconscious minds or brains, so we do not have to deal with the effects of our negative/destructive/non-optimum programming loops, which run rampant through our brains. All of these things give us power over our brain's personal computers!"

Taking full advantage of her platform to speak, Ann excitedly continued, "Which one of these modalities do you feel is the most effective? I guess you are going to say maybe different things for varying situations, but I can well imagine you are probably most partial to your "Theta Consciousness Reprogramming" and your "Theta Consciousness Healing." "Right, James?"

James loved the banter which so easily happened between he and Ann and heartily laughed as he replied, "You would be "right-e-o" in your assessments, Ann, really so right! All the modalities you talked about will work. Neuro Linguistic Programming (NLP) can be used very quickly to eliminate unwanted experiences and situations from your life via "The Swishing Technique" as per the diagram we put in *A Map to Healing and Your Essential Divinity Through Theta Consciousness*! You know, Ann, the beauty and confirmation of these things we have been talking about how we literally create everything in our lives comes from the scientific discipline of Quantum Mechanics. So while many people say science has nothing to do with religion and God, I would conjecture that what we are finding is just the opposite... **science has everything to do with God and what happens in our lives!** The marginalizing of science will not fly anymore, ha-ha, caw, caw, like a crow, which can fly better than the demeaning and "dissing" of science!

Setting his frivolity aside, James continued, "In the end, everything has to do with where you locate your energy and how you direct it. That means if I see something, I really visualize it, I focus my energy there on and allow it to come into realization in my life. Additionally, if I further visualize the magnetic charges of the plus charge on myself and negative charge on what I want to manifest, I can bring such into reality... to fruition! It really does not matter is you reverse the magnetic charges but just that we use the opposite charges, which then attract each other and bring things together! Imagine that!"

James added, "It was the "double slit" experiment that finally opened the Quantum Mechanics idea that we create what we experience, on all the various levels of our Earth experience. When this experiment was first conducted, a beam of light was directed through a middle slit in a faceplate and then an observer or participant possessing the power of  visualization saw the light directed in two beams on either side of the original slit. All this was done with only the intent of the observer!"

"I fervently believe what should be taken from this is if you want to obtain the state of immortality of your body, you must see such and know it is possible as per *Vav Vav Lamed*, the 43rd Name of God, meaning making the impossible possible and to create a condition of perfection, as per *Aleph Kaf Aleph*, the 7th Name of God!

Seeking to contribute to the conversation, Ann added, "The trick here, actually the task at hand, is to be able to focus the energy of the Creator/Prana/Chi/God/Life Force so we become so specifically directed we can then power ourselves into a focused concentration and catalyze the immortality quest into a realized conclusion. In fact, we are already very perfectly formulated human-Divine forms. We have simply lost the sight and focused realization of this. As Rabbi Yehuda Berg says in *The 72 Names of God: Technology for the Soul*, we are already perfect before we incarnate here on Earth. But we come down to Earth to play a game, ignorant of our divinity because the memory of such has been taken from us, and then we search to find this perfect self again on Earth. Many might say, especially including Hindus and Buddhists, we complete this search multiple times... until we figure out and manifest our perfection and climb off The Wheel of Karma."

"Again, it comes down to the concept there is no age in immortals as Robert Coon relates in *The Way of the Phoenix*. He further states all immortals are constantly being created from the infinite ecstasy and possibilities of the Eternal Now."

"Really, this is such wonderful and precise way of putting things as it relates to immortality. And we could also equate "The Intelligent Cosmic Vibration" from *The Bhagavad Gita* with "The Eternal Now." I just really hope, most fervently, more wise Elders get turned on to this concept because of the need to change the perceptions and ways of society on Earth! Its power is depicted in *Beyond The Mists of Time: When Trees Ruled the Earth And The Ensuing Ecstasy That Ensued*, how the Elders in the ancient civilizations were the glue and guiding force of a state of "Heaven on Earth." Sexual ecstasy; highly creative artistic expressions such as music, dance and art; scientific breakthroughs; and deep spiritual expressions and deep states of meditation, such as Kriya Kundalini

Pranayam, were the normal everyday occurrences in very ancient India, Sumeria (ancient Iraq and Iran) and Lemuria (in the Polynesian Pacific area), Atlantis and Egypt!

James further contemplated, "So as Robert Coon portrays, "... the infinite ecstasy and possibilities of The *Eternal Now*, and I know this would include *The Intelligent Cosmic Vibration*, regularly led many people *into* the innate and inherent state of immortality and these extended lifetimes created a mindset of "Heaven on Earth" and "Aleph Kaf Aleph" and the perfect state of Divine Creation that ensued there from!

Ann then responded, "That is so right, James, especially from my perspective in the highest realms of Heaven. Everything here is in a super suspended state, meaning the state of death has been transcended by a hyper-field of Divine Energy, which you and I regularly called Prana/Chi/God/Life Force/The Intelligent Cosmic Vibration." She smiled and continued her thoughts to James, This state is best depicted diagrammatically in Valery Kondratov's, *Geometry of a Uniform Field*, as per these pictures I am mentally sending to you of the ninth dimension versus your third dimension. It is clear from these diagrams the geometries of the ninth dimension are denser, even though they are the same forms as the third dimension. And, it is this complexity that allows a hyper field of energy that makes the illusion of dense matter and death impossible to exist."

Catching the meaning in Ann's energy, James replied, "That is some heavy shiite, as it were, which might mean a consciousness anchored in the Ninth Dimension is in a super-suspended state of immortality! Yes, Ann, *es la verdad?*

Ann laughingly returned, "Duh and ha-ha, caw caw ha! Well of course I never use such terminology and I am responding within your lingo again, but yes, for sure, on your Ninth Dimension consciousness proposal. I even think Mrs. Eddy would have said such in *Science and Health with Key to the Scripture* if Kondratov's *Geometries of a Uniform Field* had been available for her perusal!

Trying to keep pace with Ann's good-humored nature, James replied, Thanks you! And spelled it out for her, "Y-E-W for your angelic perspectives and confirmations! I always used to question how our Kriya Yoga Satguru, Babaji Nagaraj, lives in his immortal body in the upper echelons of the Himalayan Mountains and not do the heavy lifting by being involved in the everyday affairs of Planet Earth. You used to always tell me, Ann, Babaji was working on the inner/energy planes of Earth to build a foundation for the "New Earth." I wonder if I can wait it out with our Satguru in the Himalayas, or whether I need to get down in the trenches. God knows, I have dug enough trenches to install sprinkler pipes, ha-ha! Just imagine! An Indigo Elder digging the trenches! Yet the Indigo children, as venerated as they are, do not seem much interested in manual labor, so someone will have to do so since sometimes you have to get down and dirty, at times, ha-ha!"

CHAPTER FIVE

Transcending the Earth Jive, Being Real
Live, and Bringing the Ninth Dimension
Consciousness into the Third/Turd
Dimension and Catalyzing the Super
Suspended State of Immortality on Earth

————— ⟡ —————

IN JAMES' QUEST it seemed there was considerable evidence of
Earth transitioning into a fourth dimensional operating system after
the Winter Solstice on December 21, 2012. This can be ascertained
from the Mayan prophecies that begin in 2013, The Hopi prophecies
and also from Indian Vedic Yugas, the last one of these revealing a
Golden Age, or Satya Yuga, of ten thousand years, as prophesied by
Krishna, more than five thousand years ago! A most interesting
thing is there are only three months difference between the Golden
Age prophecies of the Mayans and the Krishna's prediction of the
Satya Yuga Golden Age.

The couple was left with the question of whether it would be
unreasonable to assume there would be a higher consciousness
commensurate with a higher dimension on Earth in this Satya Yuga
Golden Age. For James, this was really not only was a no-brainer,
but a catalytic boost to immortalizing a human body, a more
favorable environment for such with an alignment where there is a
confluence of positive energies, not only from the Sun but the center
of the Milky Way Galaxy! Yet in reality, it was not necessary to
even assume such, since more Prana is unleashed during these

Golden Ages... and more Prana equals more energy, which equates to higher dimensions operating on Earth, and this is coming from at least two sources James mentioned earlier!

As their hearts were conjoined, so were their minds; both James and Ann simultaneously pondered the significant collected evidence of increased hyper dimensional/torsional energies, which have been coming to Earth from the center of the Milky Way Galaxy since the middle 1970's, recorded by French and Russian scientists. Mutually, their thoughts landed on memories of Richard Hoagland, of The Enterprise Mission, who had also researched these powerful energies and measured their intensity, likewise. The energies have to do with a direct galactic alignment with Earth and the center of the Milky Way Galaxy! Atoms that are exposed to more energy move at a faster rate and this faster rate creates higher dimensions on Earth, at least the fourth dimension and likely even the fifth dimension!

Then of course, there is another thing affecting planet Earth and this is the Sun becoming hotter, as explained in *Removing the Shackles* published in *Dr. Robert Newton's Blog,* on Facebook. This article explains that as the Earth becomes warmer, it begins to transition into this fourth dimensional operating system. More heat also equals faster moving atoms, and the atoms have more spin, resulting in an energy that further creates the condition for the manifestation of higher dimensions; higher dimensions being where the process of immortality occurs. So it is self evident that anything that takes us into the higher dimensions, such as meditation and mantras, is capable of taking us into the realm of immortality.

So as James contemplated myriad elements of immortality, he ticked through all the thoughts gathering in his head, as he thought, *So if we add the heat factor of the Sun and the increased torsional energies of the center of the Milky Way Galaxy, what we have is atoms that move at a faster rate of vibration and spin. And as the atoms move faster, it facilitates the fourth dimension establishment with more complex geometries on the atomic level of creation on Earth. And as the Earth atoms move faster, so do our personal atoms, likewise, and so we are concurrently lifted into the fourth and even higher dimensional shifts, eventually ending in the ninth dimension and possibly going beyond that! But by the time you are in the ninth dimension, you have reached the level of the "high heavens" and all vestiges of the illusion of dense matter completely disappear and hence an immortal self is easily manifested! It really is that simple, undeniably for me!"*

As happy as he was with this revelation, James knew there were more things to add to the "immortality stew" upon which he expounded, taking up conversation once again with Ann. "Over time, the Kriya Kundalini Pranayam I do everyday causes a dimensional shift in my consciousness, after which which feel a body that is lighter, weight wise, and with a higher light quotient, and expanded mental and creative functions, which are increased beyond anything I could have imagined or hoped for! A study in 2014 by The University of Northern Arizona, clearly indicated theta brainwaves from deep level meditation; however, they did not establish a direct connection between the theta brainwaves and higher consciousness and higher dimensions. Yet inevitably... they go together."

"The fact they can measure theta brainwaves indirectly indicates a higher dimensional functioning through the increased creativity and deeper problem solving associated with these brainwaves! And of course, brainwaves, "rain waves", the brainwave is only a bio-indicator of a higher level of consciousness and not the consciousness itself! And what is even cooler is Kriya Kundalini Pranayam; besides theta consciousness will take a subject into upper delta brainwaves/ consciousness when they enter the breathless state of Samadhi. For sure, Dr. Newton and I thoroughly covered all of this and the distinction between brainwaves and higher consciousness in *A Map to Healing and Your Essential Divinity Through Theta Consciousness*."

Thinking about the project with Dr. Newton, James sat back, closed his eyes, and allowed his thoughts to go deeper. *Let's say regular meditation takes us into alpha brainwaves/consciousness into the fourth dimension... deep meditation and Pranayam takes us into the fifth dimension and theta brainwaves/consciousness... and Samadhi yields a journey into the sixth dimension and delta brainwaves/consciousness... at the end of the day, that still leaves*

51

three more dimensions before we can access the ninth dimensional level. However, when we enter Soruba Samadhi, which is a permanent state of the breathless state of Samadhi, we can transit into any dimension we desire... surely that will allow us to easily access the ninth dimension and more! Just being able to NDE in Samadhi, is cool, in and of itself... and a blessing and a gift as well!

Ann, intuiting James' thoughts then chimed in, "Well James, Mr. Smarty Samadhi Pants, you have figured out how to visit me at will, have you not? Did you already know this or did you just figure it out now?

Laughing exuberantly James replied, "I think I knew it already but did not know I knew it, ha-ha! But either way, it is irrelevant as long as things are revealed to me as I need them and since I am on the scent of immortality at this point in time, I guess I really need this because a deteriorating body is *no bueno*... well, at least for *mua*! What is being revealed here is in regular Samadhi, some of us can easily transition our consciousness into the ninth dimension and communicate with beings there from! That should blow a few minds, at the very least!

Ann quickly responded, "Well, I could not agree with you more and the radio show with Danny Caputi on *The Real Conspiracies with Scientific and Spiritual Solutions* radio show was helpful in a tangential manner. He was the doctoral candidate in mathematics and presenter at the Science and Non-Duality Conference (SAND) and opened a lot of minds to the possibility we can prove our immortality with mathematics. While Caputi doesn't prove the immortality of the physical body, at least he proves the immortality of the **essence of us**, in a mathematical sense, but then again, I live with this knowledge everyday! As Caputi says, 'The perception of the irreducible self makes us immortal,' so I guess the perception of our immortality makes us indestructible at an essential level! But you need more than that to remain on Earth as an immortal Indigo Elder!"

James then replied, "Duh, you are so very right, I do need more and fortunately for me, ha-ha, I have such and have already covered much of it in this book I am writing with Dr. Newton. But really, Ann, you are spending a lot of time down here. Are things really that boring in the ninth dimension or do you just miss the wacky me, of the most smarty of pants?"

"You know, even beyond Danny Caputi, we also have Mark Anthony's, *Evidence of Eternity: Communicating with Spirits to Prove an Afterlife*. Herein, Anthony Carr, a well-known psychic, uses information from his psychic readings of clients to give substantial anecdotal evidence of our eternal status and how we are re-united with our loved ones after we pass over to the other side. This kind of reminds me our relationship, Ann, except we freely communicate even though I have not passed over to the other side."

Ann poked James back when she relayed this, "Well, actually both things you said are accurate. And I know you miss me as much as I miss you. But, as you covered in *An Angel not Perceived*, based on my life, my mission from Heaven to Earth was actually supposed to be over almost fifteen years before I returned to Heaven. But I know what you are trying to do, enter a state of body immortality, is a monumental task... and then some, just because of the negative thoughts of humanity regarding this, stored in the morphogenic field (a field of energy resulting from the aggregated thoughts of humans) of energy, on Earth! You and I both know the very process of Kriya Kundalini Yogi, Babaji Nagaraj, was very demanding and arduous! Two Satgurus, both Boganathur and Agastyar put him through his paces."

James replied, "Undoubtedly, you are correct and fortunately for me, I never shrink away from a difficult task and beyond that, I never think about or consider the demise of my body. Additionally, as you well know, each person who pulls off this immortality gig, makes it easier for those who try to accomplish such, at a later time, as per Ken Keyes' book, *The Hundredth Monkey*, mentioned several times previously!"

"But to get back on task, we know Sun gazing is another way to increase the pranic force/Chi/God-life force in the body and expand our consciousness and access the higher dimension of theta in the fifth dimension, and delta in the sixth dimension! A lot of people consider Sun gazing to be just sheer silliness and yet after this practice you can use dowsing rods to measure the increased

Prana in the body. When you combine Sun Gazing with Kriya Kundalini Pranayam, it focuses a lot of Prana inside the head and lungs; this can be transported by circulating blood throughout the human body, which reaps the benefit thereof."

"As Dr. Newton and I covered in *A Map to Healing and Your Essential Divinity Through Theta Consciousness,* the blood circulates oxygen, which is bonded with Prana or The Intelligent Cosmic Vibration, transferred throughout the body, and combined with our theta brainwaves, transporting a person to at first the fourth dimension and then the fifth dimension and in some cases, to the sixth dimension, where space and time become irrelevant to a large degree! The key is getting to that ninth dimension, or at least close thereto, so we attain the state of pure energy, devoid of any vestiges of dense matter!"

James spent a few more minutes wrapped in his mind before he continued, "The fact we know life goes on, whether we remain in one body or transit into other bodies of various sorts, as in death, is comforting and proves in some manner we are connected, irresistibly, to The Light/God as per the 59th Name of God, *Hey Resh Chet.* There have been a lot of people who have had near death experiences (NDE's) but some really vivid descriptions of such come from Dr. Eben Alexander, a Harvard neuro-surgeon who experienced so called death and yet was completely cognizant of the surgeons who were trying to bring him back to life. He described in detail the surgical procedures over seven days that were performed on him as a result of bacterial meningitis."

James recalled when Alexander was reported to have returned from the dead, his previous agnostic stance on immortality of the soul was greatly changed to being very certain of such, but it also revealed our bodies do not have to deteriorate, even considering the so-called 120 year maximum life spans God supposedly mandated in "Exodus" of *The Torah/Old Testament.*

Mind spinning, James almost shouted in his passion, "So the idea *is* being proffered by scientists that the telomere strands of our DNA keep wearing out and DNA needs to be repaired and replicated, and these strands irretrievably shorten and we then eventually die there from. This can definitely be challenged as mere theory rather than absolute fact, **because the new facts we are being exposed to, say so!**

"Also, Marcos Berrios shared a similar description of the NDE experience, after he was burned over ninety percent of his body and supposedly died. Again, he could relay in detail just what the surgeons were doing to revive him. And even more incredible, he healed all the burns on his body without any skin grafts. Dr. Newton shared Berrios' story on his *Real Conspiracies with Spiritual and Scientific Solutions* radio show on Blog Talk radio. Maybe the show is still archived there or on SR Broadcasting."

Having given James plenty of space to talk and honoring what he had to say, Ann then shared her perspectives, "What you have revealed is really insightful and even more so in being very useful in your quest. But what is even cooler than that is you already know what you have to do get your body to a ninth dimension consciousness and actually reside in said dimension, even though you are on Earth, ha-ha! So let's concentrate on performing assiduous amounts of Kriya Kundalini Pranayam and the Sanskrit Mantras such as Aum, Gayatri and Mahamrityunjaya and other sounds with highly cymatic or vibrational properties, spiritual sexuality, and substances which cause the necessary shifts in consciousness."

James enthusiastically responded, "I am up for the discipline required for this task and am" ready to rumble!" And as far as sexuality goes, I am ready to rumba, too. But the sexual discussion will be certainly controversial as we have Tantric Sexuality which says sexuality can foster enlightenment contrasted with *The Bhagavad Gita* and Kriya Kundalini Yoga Satguru, Babaji Nagaraj, in *The Death of Death*, saying immortality can only be achieved through chastity."

"That will be a real hard sell telling a Scorpio, like Mr. Smarty Pants, James, that spiritual sexuality and Tantra are a barrier to immortality, right, James? Let the fun begin!"

James, feigning he did not hear Ann responded, "Huh?

CHAPTER SIX

Getting Ready to Rumble, Not Bumble,
and Rumba to Wit!
Immortality Within the Parameters
of Sexual and Vibrational Energy

———— ⚹ ————

JAMES WAS DEFINITELY thinking about the Rumba and the many wonders and dimensional shifts possible through the right application of sexual energies. But he was led to focus first on the vibrational factors of the Sanskrit language and mantras, the sacred sounds of Hebrew, the cymatic or vibrations of the Egyptian Hieroglyphs, The Solfeggio frequencies, signing, toning, the musical perpetual motion machines of John Keely and the diatonic scale healing modalities of Sound Signature protocols as set forth by Sharry Edwards. Fortunately or unfortunately, James was strongly influenced by Ann using a type of Martian Mind Meld or telepathic connection with James. This was something that came naturally between them, anyway.

Ann, laughingly asserted, "Well, Mr. Smarty Pants Scorpio, I know you would rather consider the sexual energies and their transformative effect sooner rather than later. But I feel intuitively we should cover the vibration/cymatic aspects of how they change so-called matter by bombarding such with energy and thus making it more like spirit/energy rather than the illusive form of dense matter, so widely accepted as true! But again, there are vibrational aspects to sexuality! Who'd of thunk such?"

"Well, then, Ann, we will do things your way, as I have found you are usually right about just about everything. So we have already talked about "Aum/Om" and how the vibrations from this word create at least eight geometry forms on the atomic level of existence. And we also know *The Gayatri Mantra* elicits similar results on the atomic level by creating the form of *The Shree Yantra*. So when we get into these atomic geometries, the more complex they are, and the two examples above are complex, the higher the dimensions we can access and the immortality attached thereto."

James mind momentarily fixed on the figure, which is the affect of Aum, and shows an atomic complexity and a high dimensional expression, and that of the *Shree Yantra*, which his conversation with Ann stimulated.

Bringing his mind back to their shared conversation, James continued, "So a picture is worth at least a thousand words, and many times worth a million words. In the case of Hebrew, the research of Dr. Hans Jenny revealed the Hebrew vowels will be replicated on a plate of sand and he saw the same effect in Sanskrit! In *Sacred Letters and Sacred Numbers Hebrew and Sacred Geometry*, there is a discussion of how the cymatic/ vibrational properties of the Hebrew alphabet and numbers affect our DNA and cells through their affect on the amino acids within the DNA and all this relates to healing and changing the human body, which seems to be a lot less human than we have been bamboozled into believing and **much more composed of atoms, energy, with a natural immortalized state!** These exact Hebrew letters are what comprise *The 72 Names of God*, from Exodus 14, Verses 19-21, of *The Torah*. This is similar to what Masaru Emoto the Japanese researcher, who claimed that human consciousness—our thought and sound—has an effect on the molecular structure of water, and is thought to produce geometric forms in water. What a coincidence, Ann."

Surprisingly, not just happily agreeing with James as he had grown accustomed, Ann then forcefully replied, "Cha wrong! Planned coincidence yes, but random coincidence, no way, Jose! These letters of Hebrew, be they chosen by the Jewish Rabbis or more likely by the Sumerians/Anunaki, were specifically chosen so that so called dense matter could be transformed into its real essence of energy! These are the types of forms that proliferate here in the ninth dimension of the highest realms of Heaven, but you already figured this out, James! There is even an interesting theory the Hebrew language came from our binary pairs DNA code. **Maybe there are cymatic properties and/or music associated with DNA!** I think it is more likely rather than less so! Things just keep getting more interesting and clarified!"

"Indeed, the power of *The 72 Names of God,* in Hebrew, can be seen by the atomic forms created there from, so we have the strongest evidence that things, including our bodies, can be modified and optimized by these forms below. Part of that optimization is the immortalization of our bodies!

James continued, "This type of cymatic transformation is also found in the Solfeggio Frequencies, a "lost scale," different from our diatonic scale and much more powerful. In fact, this scale was used in the composition of the Gregorian chants and probably accounts for their ethereal quality! These notes are more powerful because they have a higher cymatic force and result. There was a time when this was widely known, but with the diatonic scale this knowledge was buried, lost, or maybe even suppressed! The water crystal pictures taken of the Solfeggio scale look eerily similar to some of Dr. Emoto's water crystal pictures. Certainly, listening to

 music in tones of the Solfeggio scales would be most transformative and even revitalizing of the human body and a factor in immortalizing a body. Just look at the pictures now filtering through my mind, Ann!

"The six main Solfeggio Frequencies are where magic happens, as in the magic of immortality! So listening to and toning the frequencies below could change us big time, Ann! How

these relate to the Schuman Resonance Earth Frequency at 7.83 Hz, I have not ascertained as yet. Is there something I am missing? And in fact there is something I am missing as Nick Anthony Fiorenza states in "432hz and Schuman Resonance. As Fiorenza relates, 8hz = the note C4 = 256hz = A4 = 430.54 hz and so there is a very close math between 7.83 hertz and a Solfeggio musical note! "Considering the Schuman Resonance can actually vary between 7hz-8.5hz, there is a resonance between these things, at least some of the time."

"I have the strongest feeling the power of the Solfeggio Frequencies have been **deliberately hidden from us** so as to obscure this immortality protocol and leave us in a state of ignorance and inevitable death! In *Healing codes for the Biological Apocalypse,* Horowitz and Puleo talk about the rejuvenating properties of the Solfeggio Frequencies. So while the idea might be considered as nothing more than random babble by many people it is more like a certifiable proof, taking this concept out of mere speculation!"

"Additionally, there is a lot of evidence the Schuman Resonance if being negated by electromagnetic pollution from the alternating current of not only our electricity grid but from our electrical devices and technologies. This can lead to an interference with cell division and our overall health, with a number of health issues related thereto! Paul Brodeur, the investigative science writer of *Currents of Death*, discusses the topic in depth in the book. Obviously, this would have implications to immortalizing our existing bodies! Lo and behold, toning or playing the Solfeggio Frequencies will counter the diminutions of the Schuman Resonance and the assault on our cells, and can be a catalyst into a state of an immortalized human body! It seems the Solfeggio Frequencies would program the human brain/mind to an optimum state and remove negative/counter productive brain programming."

Ann added her input, "Wow, just imagine what might happen if you toned these frequencies throughout the day. For sure there is an inter-relationship between them and the Chakra/energy centers in the body and human emotions and health."

James replied, "Undoubtedly, this is true and it also brings us to Sharry Edward's, "Sound Signature Therapy" and using sub woofer notes to heal the human body and mollify our emotions. And it is interesting how Edwards has ascertained almost all people have at least one note in the diatonic scale, which is missing from the vocal patterns/notes emanating from their speech patterns. It has been Edward's contention by rebuilding that missing note from a person voice, health and disease problems will disappear. So I would interject then, would this aid in immortality of our existing bodies?"

Ann's mind was as fertile with ideas as was James' and she added, "Then you have the most amazing musician, John Keely, who created machines that would run perpetually on a "fuel" of diatonic scale musical notes. Keely called the power of these notes, Aether. So why could you not run your body in a state of perpetuity in a similar manner as the machines, via this Aether? How would you do this? Most likely through a state of continual signing and Sanskrit mantras, a kind of praying without ceasing, as Mary Baker Eddy revealed in *Science and Health with Key to the Scriptures*."

"You could probably get the same result with those toning techniques we learned in The Tibetan Foundation, especially with the vocal vowel sounds and the results found on the atomic level with the Hebrew and Sanskrit languages! Probably the best example of this is the recordings by David Hykes and the Harmonic Choir such as *On Hearing Solar Winds*. It is such an amazing reflection of the power and usefulness of the human voice, but not just through the normal notes of the diatonic scale! And of course, your recording of Aum, *The Gayatri Mantra* and *The Mrityunjaya Mantra* are equally as powerful and effective as *On Hearing Solar Winds*, James."

James quickly replied, "All those vocal things are powerful and I loved recording my mantra CD! The concepts of Keely were thoroughly covered in *The Journal of Sympathetic Vibratory Physics,* produced by Dale Pond and other contributors to this journal. Jerry Decker has also covered these things in Keely Net. This avenue of vibrations/cymatic is rife with opportunities, as I see it and truly an integral part of the immortality protocols."

Ann suddenly recalled Hans Couseau's, *The Cosmic Octave*, where he discusses the healing and rejuvenating properties of the diatonic scale, and asked James, "Does it seem, from Couseau's work that scales, notes, octaves and the vibrational properties related thereto, whether they be diatonic or Solfeggio, are our "friends"+, raising our consciousness to higher dimensions and rejuvenating us and extending our life spans?"

"Also, I would like to bring up the effect of negative ion generators, be they manmade or natural. There are negative ion generators that are manufactured and they really make a positive effect on humans, by making us feel better, through the negative electrical charges they release. More importantly, there are many sources of natural negative ions such as the crashing water from waves, rapids, waterfalls and Quartz and other piezoelectric minerals like Topaz and Tourmaline. And just being in Nature, removes us from our industrialized cities with a surplus of depressing, positive ions...just another catalyst in the immortality quest. But now, Mr. Smarty Pants would like to address the controversial sexuality approach to immortality!"

"I should mention first, however, you have the negative ion generation combined with far infrared rays in the Richway "Bio-mat". And the power of combining these things, with a low voltage power source, not only removes pain, makes people sleep better, and removes cancer from the human body, it also helps stabilize the body in the higher state of Pran/Chi/God-life force! **Now** Mr. Smarty Pants would like to address the controversial sexuality approach to immortality!"

Really getting into things, James stated, "We are getting back to one of my favorite subjects, spiritual sexuality! Now it says in *The Bhagavad Gita* and Babaji Nagaraj, *The Death of Death,* **immortality of our existing bodies can only be achieved in a state of chastity!** And yet we have Tantric Sexuality in such texts as *The Kama Sutra* and ancient Taoist knowledge of sexuality, such as *Tao of Sexology: Sexual Wisdom and Methods,* by Dr. Stephen T. Chang and *History of Sacred Sexuality,* by Michael Mirdad, the spiritual teacher.

"Many of ancient Taoist texts considered only providing longevity for the man in a sexual relationship and the woman was only a means of sharing her energy with the man, even though her sexual satisfaction was considered important. From what I have learned, **leaving the woman behind is counterproductive as you are ignoring the receptive feminine energy!**" Even Kriya Kundalini Yoga Satguru, Thirumoolar, considered woman as vampires of a man's energy, in his book, *Thirumandiram*! However, not only is this extremely chauvinistic, it is outright selfish and ignores The Laws of Karma. Yet if the woman catalyzes the Agna and Yagna or fire and light in the man during a sexual conjoining, it is imperative the man reciprocate and share his energy with his woman during his orgasm and pull her into the higher dimensions, also. "

"In Tantra and Taoism, it is clearly stated, numerous times, when a man ejaculates his sperm he is depleting himself, since there is Prana/chi being released in the semen. So you must contract the anal sphincter muscles so as to stem the outflow of the semen at the perineum. This actually can decrease the force, energy and pleasure when the man climaxes, and it also blocks the Prana of the woman being fully shared with her partner, from heart to heart. So what if we men were able to recapture and increase the Prana we lose through sharing our semen through the energy circuits we can create when we open our heart to our woman? In fact none of the Tantra or Taoists texts ever mention this. So apparently I need to mention it, ha-ha!"

Ann laughingly responded, "Well, James, I have never known you to keep quiet about anything you have discovered, regardless of the consequences. I must say, it is interesting how you have pointed out virtually no texts have considered the reciprocal energy the woman can and actually does share with the man, during a sexual union. I know you agree with me about Kriya Kundalini Yoga Sadguru Thirumoolar insulting comments about women being "energy vampires" as inaccurate, even though he is an exalted Guru! The mind shattering energies you and I created in our sexual unions used to keep us in an altered consciousness for hours, with many cutting edge insights into esoteric and scientific matters! This is well revealed in "The Kundalini Sex Brain Picture."

James smiled as he replied, "Yes, the energies we created were certainly special, as you relate. I did release my semen and never felt depleted and actually, to the contrary, very energized, often in the breathless state of Samadhi, and definitely ensconced in lower theta and upper delta brainwaves and the ensuing higher consciousness related thereto."

Ann quickly added, "**I guess we have evidence to the contrary which indicates "chastity" is not absolutely necessary to reach the deepest realms of God/the higher dimensions accessed therein**! So I would say you could enter permanent state of breathlessness of the human body that Yogi Govindan always referred to as Soruba Samadhi. Imagine that, James!"

"I am already imagining such and so I am freed from the chastity of Brahmachari! Anyway, how could there be any shortage of Prana/Chi/God-life force since The Intelligent Cosmic Vibration permeates everything, as stated in *The Bhagavad Gita* and we are always connected to the light, as per *Hey Resh Chet*, the 59th *Name of God?* The atoms that comprise all energy, of an electromagnetic type, never get tired, never wear out, and never get depleted! Therefore, neither do I, since I am made from these amazing atoms and lucky for me, this is what is, ha-ha!"

Additionally, there is ample evidence in ancient Egypt from the hieroglyphs, the Egyptians viewed sex as necessary for rebirth into the after life. Not to mention, the *Kama Sutra* and Taoist texts have the purpose of propelling the male into a state of immortality, as a result of sexual conjoining. So people can call me a "spiritual perve" if they must, yet they must get their facts and concepts straight before they can do so with any real meaning, ha-ha! Did I mention I am laughing my ass off?"

CHAPTER SEVEN

*Getting Closer to Heaven and
Bringing a State of Leaven to
Immortalize the Human Body*

───── ❖ ─────

AS JAMES CONTEMPLATED this he realized he had many
leavening substances that are catalysts to bring the body into the
immortal state in which is was conceived! He thought, *It is safe to
say the Anunaki used octahedron shaped substance of Gold to
extend their life spans into the thousand year time frames they
experienced. I believe this was called Ormus, a monatomic form of
Gold/God that when it is ingested, raises the vibrations/energy
potential of humans, animals and plants! And today, this Ormus can
be purchased and used to attain the same results accessed by the
Anunaki, the ET's who inhabited Sumer (ancient Iran/Iraq),
450,000 years ago and at various other times, likewise. Yet of the
people I know who use Ormus, I do not see as intense auras around
them like depicted around Yeshua/Jesus, but then again, that might
not be a realistic comparison.*

James knew there is a significant Prana/Chi/God life force
enhancement through the use of Ormus and many studies had
shown the energy and life spans of rats was measurably increased
from the ingestion thereof. He had seen these same Pranic energies
in the auras of people who do assiduous amounts of Kriya Kundalini
Pranayam breathing meditation and Sanskrit mantras, especially
Aum, *The Gayatri Mantra*, and *The Maha Mrityunjaya Mantra*.
Suddenly, James focused on a very strong commitment, *Anything*

like Ormus, which I have not been using... from this day forward I need to and will be ingesting and rubbing on my body. Anything that will give me "a kick in the ass" will propel me in the direction of immortality! Once again verbalizing his thoughts, in order to make sure he was able to share them with Ann, Robert said, "Anything that gives you a boost into immortality cannot be bad! For sure, we have Zecharia Sitchin originally to thank for having sufficient information about Ormus. I have received a lot more from Barry Carter, who is an expert who was on Dr. Newton's Real Conspiracies with Scientific and Spiritual Solutions radio show."

Ann taking her time to assess the situation, replied, "Well, I remember our friend, Ron, took the Ormus and said it made subtle changes in him. But I know you are a firm believer and user of hot pepper tincture. You know I found that stuff just way to brutal to ingest!"

"Ah! "I remember how much you disliked the Cayenne tincture, yet I am sure it could have stopped the vaginal bleeding that led to your death. I know I avoided hot substances like the plague until I learned about the amazing benefits of the capsaicin, the substance that makes the hot peppers "hot", from Dr. Richard Schulze. After learning you could stop a heart attack or stroke or remove a blood clot with cayenne and habanero pepper tincture, and then I found out you can cure cancer with these hot pepper tinctures, as well as a cold and influenza, my perspective became significantly changed."

"I realized I needed to convince myself to start using this to get the amazing benefits thereof! And so that is just what I manifested in my life! Then I started getting intuited information about how these hot peppers were attractors and transporters of Prana/Chi/God-life force throughout the body and I became even more enamored with and used even more of the hottest pepper tincture I could find, specifically habanero. I also started using more hot peppers as an accoutrement to the main dishes I was eating. Now there are hot peppers more than twice as hot as the habanero."

"Of course it helped I learned how to make these tinctures myself by grinding the pepper with Vodka. I ingest two eye droppers full of habanero tincture everyday and use it on my spinal column and neck and back, so as to act as an amplifier and transporter of Prana throughout my body. We know the spinal column can attract and move vast amounts of Prana/Chi and distribute it throughout the body! The effect of this, inside and outside the body is, in fact, quite intense. When you apply it exteriorly, it will be very hot on the body for hours at a time so this is not a treatment for wusses"

James knew Ann already understood that what happens is the capsaicin in the peppers moves the blood faster through the body and thus moves the Prana faster. Again, when the Prana/atoms move faster... the body becomes less material and more its real form of energy. This is the result of the body being pulled into higher dimensions. The higher the dimension, the more the energy and the less the dense materialness of the body manifests itself. Anything that can do all the things cayenne and habanero pepper can do, is something immensely powerful, and thus worthy of consideration as a catalyst to immortalize the human body.

Not to consider herself in the category of a "wuss," Ann responded, "With the knowledge you always shared with me, I know these hot peppers are indeed powerful, but I always tended to favor the Tulsi/Holy Basil/Occinum Sanctum tea we used to drink, and the capsules of Holy Basil we took from New Chapter supplement. I know it is a good medicine for colds and influenza, also. But for your purposes, it is the tranquilizing and relaxing properties of Tulsi that will help you in your quest for immortality of your body because a relaxed body is a body, which can allow more Prana/Chi course into the body and be more fully distributed there about! I know you, James, being a Tai Chi master, understand that when relaxed you can move the body without muscle power and solely through Chi."

James, clearly understanding Ann's remarks, replied, "I know what you mean Ann! The Tulsi will relax my body more and maybe even to the point where I become so filled with Prana/Chi/light **I will transfigure my body in a Merkabah/body of light and thus be indestructible and immortalized!** I remember the time I was in the class with Tim Latimer, a great Tai Chi Chuan teacher, with three other people and we had beads of sweat rolling down our faces in an air conditioned twenty foot by twenty foot room from just doing the Tai Chi Standing Meditation for a full twenty minutes. I am sure you know, Ann, there is no movement in the standing meditation and no physical exertion, just deep relaxation, so the heat that caused the sweat could only have been from the Chi/Prana/God-life force we attracted and distributed throughout our bodies and the room! **The slower our breathing, the more we relaxed and the more Prana/Chi we created hence more heat and more sweat.** I wonder what would happen if I put an eye dropper or two of cayenne or habanero tincture in my Tulsi tea or the Tulsi tincture I have formulated?"

Ann laughingly replied, "You can have that "poison" yourself, James, since it is way too hot for me but since you are such a "hot tamale," there could be some interesting results if you combine Tulsi with hot pepper tincture, ha-ha! I would, however, not mind taking the ASEA, the stabilized formula comprised of Redux cells, you have been taking."

James tauntingly replied, "So you will not take the hot pepper tincture, but you will take the Tulsi and ASEA, will you? Actually, you have no need for any of these things since in your angelic form you are manifested in a Merkabah! That Merkabah light body serves you well, Ann, making you even more beautiful than I remember you being! With the ASEA, I know the Redux cells are rejuvenating my body but possibly the bigger benefit is how the Redux cells anchor your consciousness in the Theta brainwaves and the higher consciousness that comes there with. Because it is being in that constant higher consciousness that is part and parcel of being able to figure out this immortality metamorphosis and the transfiguration which comes with that!"

Ann replied with certainty, "James, your openness to trying these things has always amazed me. You are pickier with some foods but when longevity is involved, you have always been on "the cutting edge." I remember the John Ellis Water Machine, which takes water and makes H2O2 (Hydrogen Peroxide) in a way it can be drunk. And drink it you did! For me, that peroxide taste was unpalatable but for you it was ingestible! Go figure, huh? But what this also indicates is Hydrogen Peroxide itself, is a component of immortality. But I really need to emphasize, people really need to understand Hydrogen Peroxide and should read Ed McCabe's book, *Oxygen Therapies,* before they use it."

"And you know, James of the Smartest Pants, we should not forget about using Stabilized Oxygen as part of the Alchemical use of Oxygen, to immortalize the body. Whether the Oxygen comes from the John Ellis Water Machine or from various sources of Hydrogen Peroxide or the stabilized Oxygen, we know when Oxygen bonds to Prana/Chi/God-Life force, it transports it throughout the human body, and the energy characteristics of that body will be greatly enhanced. And we both know Stabilized Oxygen is easy to ingest and to take with you when you are out during the day and away from home."

James pondered the past few moments of their conversation be fore he responded, "In my case, I learn to like things that like me; that help me. And I know, as per the book I did with Dr. Newton, *A Map to Healing and Your Essential Divinity Through Theta Consciousness,* that Oxygen carries Prana/Chi/God-Life force throughout the human body. It is that Prana, and the not oxygen itself, that sustains our bodies. Yet I have more to consider because adding the extra hydrogen atom to the water makes it amazing in ways I may not completely understand, but I am realize hydrogen is also a transporter of Prana/Chi/God-life force throughout our bodies."

"There is also this water from Japan that has extra hydrogen added to it. I think this Hydrogen factor starting making more sense when I was exposed to "Mantle Dynamics," on LinkedIn and Ronald Patrick Marriot, curator of the Mantle Dynamics page, was explaining the importance of Hydrogen and what it does. Then I started to realize hydrogen must be a component of Yagna, fire, and possibly even Agna, light... the very stuff we breath into the body during Kriya Kundalini Pranayam and the Intelligent Cosmic Vibration from *The Bhagavad Gita,* since hydrogen is known to support the combustion process of fire. Wow, this stuff would make a really interesting book! I wonder who might be qualified to write that book, Ann?"

Ann laughingly replied, "James, you are some damn funny. That is why I loved living with you. Intelligent, spiritual, highly creative and most of all, so ridiculously funny! Who might be qualified to write that book? LMAO, Mr. Smarty Pants!"

CHAPTER EIGHT

*Really Feeling Great,
But How Do I Rate?
Are Numbers Part Of The Immortality
Equation?
T.O.O.L.S Anyone?*

———— ·······•·•····· ————

JAMES REALIZED HE was blessed beyond what any words could express from the help of Facebook friends, who kept feeding him a constant stream of cutting edge information, which he was able to use in the books, he co-wrote with Dr. Robert Newton. These included Kay (Karen) Dring, Jack Robert Emery, Jack's Group, Lynne Folan, Dan Winter, Ramunas Alanus, Brenda j. Tenerlli Smith, Daniel Deeter, Oz Ra Zabi, Chad Knudsen, Maja Janvanovic and Dr. Janni Lloyd, who demonstrated uncommon knowledge in immortality which she shared in her books, *Immortality the Fun Way* and *Is it Possible to be Ageless?*

Beyond this however, there were the two creators of the Temple of Objective Life Study (T.O.O.L.S), Chris Dillard and Lee Ross, who were consistently blowing James' mind with their insights into the numbers behind the English alphabet and words. Quite literally, as James was contemplating all these insights he realized, *the numeral/numerical **value** of words gives us an insight into the **real meaning** of them and it is beyond amazing the clarity you get from the words themselves! But beyond this, knowing what a word like immortality **means numerically**, gives you the secret* *meanings no one else perceives and yet is there in plain sight, right in front of your face, unperceived!"*

"In the word "immortality", we have the number 101 and that coincides with the Temple of Philae in Egypt, which also means 101, as was relayed to me and Dr. Newton by Lee Ross, one of the founders of T.O.O.L.S. So when I did some more searching of the T.O.O.L.S information and some other sources I found the word "love" in Greek also equals 101. So we know then, the more filled with love we are the more easily we can gain immortality. That is especially significant, in and of itself, since 101 also equals The Son of God and the Arch Angel Michael, who is most likely the most favorite and useful Angel of God, because he is the protector for those who invoke his name! This also could indicate the love we can generate in a sexual union, is more useful than a chaste approach to sexuality. Obviously, this sex must be within the parameters of heart opening love as opposed to an orgy or fetishes. It is the approach and the intent that matter here, Ann, like what you and I consistently experienced in our romantic unions!"

"Now, I am going to go much deeper into the angel connection here, but first, I would like to point out the number one equals new beginning, creativity, creation, motivation, progress, initiative, assertiveness... and also to mention intuition, inspiration, happiness, positivity, attainment, achieving success, and personal fulfillment. Do you think these qualities might be germane to the process of attaining immortality of the human body, Ann?"

"Before you respond to that, consider there is also more to this equation, Ann, since the number zero equals God Force, Universal Energies, eternity, infinity, oneness, wholeness, continuation of cycles and flowing-ness, and a beginning point. It also equals potential and/or choice, and developing spiritual qualities. Zero further means experiencing a spiritual journey that may involve uncertainty/unpredictability. This also involves listening to our intuition, and higher self to find answers to things. So... do you think these too, might apply to the "immortality stew," Ann?

Unable to stop his queries long enough to allow Ann to answer, James interjected with yet another question, "So, Ann, this is so revealing and means the power of the 101 number literally means the word "immortality," and has the force and qualities, in and of itself, to help us enter a state of bodily immortality. We are given energy of God, which has the qualities necessary to pull this off and the means to pull do it too! So I mean... well, I really mean the word immortality itself gives us the motivation and momentum to become immortal! What think ye about all this, Ann?"

Whew, Ann thought, *I have to stop and think about the barrage of questions James just tossed at me!* Finally, in great circumspection she replied, "Well, there is no argument from me, to the contrary, on what you have said here, Mr. Smarty Pants, and there is even more I can add and it relates to angels! Now 101 *is also* the number of Angels and you just mentioned Arch Angel Michael. By using this number and the word immortality, you can invoke angels into your life and tie into their Universal Energies for personal development, spiritual awakening/enlightenment... all to accomplish your soul mission/life purpose and to elevate your vibration to attract abundance and positive energies into your life. And this can all be supplemented with positive affirmations, optimistic attitudes and laughing, to attract what you need to succeed. This transformation can come from inner wisdom, intuition and angelic guidance/counseling, Can you dig that, James?"

Ann always gave him good reason to chuckle, and James found himself laughingly responding, "I can dig that like digging a hole to planting a tree! And soon, lucky for me, I will be as free as a tree and living in a state of perpetual glee! I would further say the word immortality wants us to be immortal! Is that from the "hand of God"? I cannot prove such, but intuitively I am feeling that is true and I am using my angel intuition to ascertain such, ha-ha!"

Ann, joining in James' laughter replied, "By the way, James of the Smart Pants, your rating is off the charts after figuring out all of these things related to the word immortality which gives us the map to the actual immortality of the body! But what is the meaning of love?

With great circumspection, James replied, "That has to be the big question where everyone throws this most ambiguous word, love, around in a cavalier manner! However, by the numbers, "Love" is 54, which also equates to the Sun and the great Enoch, who transformed into a Merkabah, an immortal body of light. And of course, the Sun is the embodiment of light, so love must well include these aspects of light and fire, Agna and Yagna! And as the body becomes filled with Agna and Yagna, it assumes it Divine potential. So this then brings us to *Science and Health with Key to the Scriptures*, where Mary Baker Eddy starkly proclaimed, "God is Love," throughout her books."

James continued, "So to express Love, apparently we must express or radiate God. And we do that through our practice of Kriya Kundalini Yoga and Kriya Kundalini Pranayam, Tai Chi. It means we should repeat *The Gayatri Mantra* and *The Maha Mrityunjaya Mantra*, both salutations to the Sun/God and to manifest our connection thereto. And further, by repeating *Lamed Vav Vav,* the nineteenth Name of God, which means "dialing God" and *Hey Resh Chet*, the 59th Name of God, meaning connected to the Light, we have portals to establishing the quixotic and elusive properties of "Love." Once we anchor these things in our bodies, they are no longer quixotic, nor elusive and become firmly ensconced in our being, even our being-ness!"

Rather amazed, Ann chimed in, "That is so cool how you explained that James. Certainly, what you described, the Agna and the Yagna—the light and the fire—are an inherent part of the higher dimensions... the dimensions of heaven! Yet even here, everybody does not necessarily love or like each other, so it is a constant quest to keep "the Love vibration" established and functioning. In the end, we must completely surrender to God. This is how we "love" and there is really no other way. This is how we enter a bodily state of immortality."

After all the years they had shared, James was not surprised by Ann's conversation, but he was certainly impressed, and let Ann know. "Wow, that is so cool-mundo what you just shared, likewise, irrespective of what I discovered! But dig this, Ann! The code letters of the DNA, A-C-T-G, equal 31 and the inverse of this is 13. God equals 26 and 13 x 2 equals 26. So our DNA is quite possibly a double dose of God, a binary pair dose in a double helix. Taking this further, a double dose of God, our DNA, was most likely created in a perfect manner. So say *sayonara* to God creating flawed and imperfect DNA and imperfect beings, duh! *Caso cerrado!*"

"Certainly, there are many such cool insights into the numeral value of words in the T.O.O.L.S text, *The Hermetic Way Spiritual Alchemy Primer,* Parts I and II", James continued. Hopefully, this will turn on a lot of people, and have the scales removed from their eyes by learning about The Hermetic Way through T.O.O.L. resources.

"Now there are even more gems I have unearthed or that have been sent to me by my friends." James continued, "One thing that deals with the perpetual energy genius, Nikola Tesla, who claimed the "Key to the Universe" is reference to the numbers 3-6-9. 3+6=9 and include 1,2,3,4,5,6,7,and 8. So there is more force in these numbers. Some people believe they allow things to come into manifestation from the higher energies contained in these particular numbers. These numbers also total the sum of 18, which is also 81, and reduce themselves to 9. Nine, being the sum of all the other numbers, takes the aggregate energy and becomes the most powerful number. So with this higher inherent energy and power, can number nine be used to pierce the veil of death? It would certainly seem possible!"

Ann, not wanting to be outdone (like that would really matter to an angel being, ha-ha) then shared some things regarding numbers and related to Edward Leedskalninm, the eccentric Latvian emigrant who claimed the Secret Numbers of the Universe are 7129+610+5195 Hz (Hertz). "Minus the Hz part, these numbers aggregate to 46 and its inverse, 64. 46 ='s Palladium and we just happen to have 46 chromosomes. So we might well be able to use the power of Palladium and the chromosomes of our DNA to enter a portal to immortality. Number 46 is considered a "pure number" so such purity might also into the planes of immortality."

After dazzling each other, James and Ann glanced in a goofy manner and just started laughing. James yelled out, "Checkmate!"

Ann quickly replied, "Queen me!"

To which James sarcastically replied, I like both checks and queens and whatever they are, they are! But I know as a fact, to love more, I need to light more, to be more en-light-ened (in the light in the end)!"

CHAPTER NINE

Nature Is So Fine!
Why Do Humans Get In Such A Grind?

JAMES BROOK'S MASTERPIECE, the movie *Avatar*, was a watershed event in modern times about the values of living in harmony and sustainability with nature. It also brought to the forefront, the idea of communicating with trees and animals, although J. Boone Allen's book, *Kinship with all Life*, covered this territory many decades earlier! Yet now, we are getting scientific proof that indicates trees and plants communicate with each other and even with other animals and of course with humans who exhibit a high degree of sentience and telepathy, highly developed psychic abilities of Clairsentience (super sensing) and telepathy (mental communication)! Even more amazing, trees have been recorded issuing music from their presences!

So despite the fact many religious people feel humans are the only beings capable of thought, sentience/feeling and creativity, recent finds are basically dispelling these misperceived notions, so much so that to think of humans as superior creations of God would be an incorrect judgment and perception, in light of the evidence related thereto, using the same metrics! Both James and Ann knew these things mentioned above.

Despite their many years in Christian Science, where the founder thereof, Mary Baker Eddy, in *Science and Health with Key to the Scripture*, stated that God was not in Nature and Pantheism was a misperceived idea, James and Ann found substantial proof to the contrary. Also James' and Dr. Newton's books, especially *A Map to Healing and Your Essential Divinity Through Theta Consciousness*, in chapter twelve, and *Beyond the Mists of Time: When Trees Ruled the Earth,* both indicated fractal geometries and the perfection displayed throughout all Nature.

In *Beyond the Mists of Time: When Trees Ruled the Earth*, it was revealed how when ancient societies lived in harmony and sustainability with Nature, there was a thriving society and a happy populace and abundance and prosperity for all people instead of a privileged few, like today, but as soon as societies and individuals starting drifting away from Nature, many problems beset them, which eventually led to the demise of these civilizations! It became obvious to Ann, James and Dr. Newton, the answers to saving our civilizations was to employ the concepts of living in sustainability with Nature. This also meant eliminating corporations, innately fictitious creations, which consistently had the proclivity to hoard resources and then over charge for distribution, sale and the use thereof! This negative effect of corporations is too hard to ignore, even though you have the benefits of large-scale production and/or distribution of resources.

As James pondered all of this he was reminded of his foray into the Kings Canyon Wilderness area with his son, Robert, and how he was communicating with many old trees and even huge boulders. From the five hundred to a thousand and more years old trees, James viewed many trees that had been damaged! When viewing such, James thought, "I remember seeing the trees with cavities in their trunks caused by forest fires, lightning and even other trees crashing into them and yet they are still living even hundreds of years later. In modern Arboriculture (the study of trees), it is believed impossible for these trees to live hundreds of years in this manner and in towns; trees really do not do so. The question then is whether it is the thoughts of the trees or the thoughts of the humans who are causing an early demise of our trees in our cities?

James thoughts began to take form as he articulated them, "For sure, and repeatedly to wit, the trees with these cavities told me, when I asked them, how they could live so long in the condition that had been inflicted on them, they consistently replied mentally, 'We do not see our condition as a calamity and we just go on living, without worrying about our condition!' Then, as I compared that to humans, who when they get an injury, how they focus on it, get a diagnosis, get fearful from the diagnosis and more often than not, this makes their condition worse, the trees become vastly superior to humans in many metrics, because the subconscious/ unconscious mind always creates what it focuses upon, good or bad... beneficial or not such!

The trees somehow know how to control their thoughts, through their state of non-reaction to events. In the case of humans, they are reacting to any and all events and so suffer the negative consequences of this in decrease health and short life spans, at least in comparison to a tree

The irony of this was not lost on James, as it were, and he thought, *I would then have to conclude this shows the superiority of the trees over humans. The tree lives considerably longer than humans, also! And although the trees do not live forever, they are also dispensing their seeds about, helped by squirrels and chipmunks. This is a mutually beneficial symbiotic relationship/a win-win situation, where the animals get food and the trees extend their lives through their progeny seedlings that germinate from their animal dispersed seeds!*

This led James to question, "Is it possible for trees to reveal things about immortalizing my human body? Certainly, their life spans in the wilds of Nature are beyond ours. There is no doubt to this! So just by the fact they remain in an extended incarnation would give them the tendency to know more things about life and immortality than I possess. Of course I have a lot of information and wisdom stored in my DNA brought through from previous incarnations, but trees may have the same thing and the longer time you can remain in an incarnation, the wiser you can become."

"For me, it is more than interesting how trees have very short life spans in towns. This may be because of damaging environmental factors, but it could also be because the negative thoughts of humanity in the cities causes the trees to have shorter lives... because of our negative energy, and/or because of our preexisting beliefs that trees in cities simply cannot live that long. It is the same mindset we personally carry that we cannot live that long, and that we must deteriorate, get sick and then die. What an old, boring and worn out scenario, duh! It is still an enigma to me that people cannot see trees are really considerably superior to humans! Certainly, Dr. Newton and I shared the many ways this happens in Chapter Twelve of *A Map to Healing and Your Essential Divinity Through Theta Consciousness.*

Just as James was about to consider more, Ann chimed in, 'Hey, Mr. Smarty Pants, you are getting a little "freaky" here and I don't know whether to blame it on you, your pants, your smartness or the smartness of your pants ha-ha! But your freakiness is leading you into fertile territory, so who am I to criticize your standard operating procedure of "thinking outside of the box"? Good God, you are thinking so far "outside of the box so as to obliterate it! You are beyond Earth and are approaching a galactic perspective, something like we had when we had those incarnations of Sirius "B" and Andromeda."

James, tugging on his smart pants replied, "Well, Ann, you know me too well and you said more than once, I am the most radical person you have ever known. I will wear that moniker with my "smart pants" with pride and distinction, ha-ha, caw, caw, hah! But really, I have no time for or interest in the "pride and distinction" baloney! Pardon my flippancy, but what if I could learn more from a tree about immortality than the Kriya Kundalini Yogis/Satgurus we studied under? Such thoughts would be considered heretical but then again, heretics are always on the cutting edge and are only marginalized because the populace at large has no idea what they are even "about" and how they operate and/or their new perspectives just make the majority of people uncomfortable."

"I know you are going to ask me just how this might happen, Ann, and I am going to mention how both Yeshua/Jesus and Moses went into the wilderness and came back very changed. Remember, "Big Mo" lived more than nine hundred years and Yeshua went into a state of immortality. The same happened with Kriya Kundalini Yoga Satguru, Babaji Nagaraj… who did the same thing two thousand years ago as he went into the wilderness to enter the immortalized state of Soruba Samadhi."

Ann interrupted, something she rarely, if ever did, "I can hardly wait to see where you are going to go with this, James. Let's get down to it!"

James quickly and wryly replied, "I wondered when you were going to ask me that and even I am wondering how I am going to tie the tree/Nature/ immortality connection together. Luckily for me, I am gaining access to the Akashic Records to answer yours and even my own questions. So let me break it down and as I tell you this, you will already know it! But anyway, remember when we were studying and practicing Buddhism, Gautama Buddha taught us desire is the root of all pain. We were taught to observe things and not react to them. And then when we studied with Kriya Kundalini Yogi, Govindan Satchidananda, he taught this same idea of detachment and how were supposed to view our lives as a movie but we are the not actor therein."

"Well, what has been revealed to me is that large trees are consummate examples of this state of non-desire and remote detachment. I heard this when I asked the trees how they could live so long with the wounds in their trunks and they basically said they did not focus on it. So it means they did not react to such! And so it is this state of non-desire/non-attachment, which is a major key in process of immortalizing the human body. So the more you are around these amazing old trees, the more you will learn via osmosis/telepathy from them! Not much more need I say about this, and by the way, trees never get caught up in this idiocy about sin, evil and getting off the wheel of karma. Because they are not involved in such and so are not affected thereby! So can we learn from the trees?"

Ann then replied, "Hey James, you actually said more on this subject than I imagined possible. Luckily for you, it was germane to the immortality gig, ha-ha! And yes, trees are our gurus/avatars!"

81

CHAPTER TEN

Leaving Behind The Idea Of
Sin And Karma
And Getting Off The Wheel Of Karma

———— ·✦· ————

JAMES AND ANN realized old trees had already removed themselves from the ideas and constraints of sin, evil and getting off the Wheel of Karma. James realized the task confronting humanity in pulling this off was dispelling the myopic notions already firmly ensconced on Planet Earth. Everyone seemed to believe in sin, evil and karma or a combination thereof, but are they real things or just a way to control and suppress people and take their God given freedoms and keep them contributing their money to the religions that promulgated these ideas!

Contemplating this brought this realization for James, "The concept of *Aleph Kaf Aleph* the seventh name of God from *The 72 Names of God* from *Exodus* in *The Torah*, meaning restoring things to their perfect state, is not much in vogue right now among the populace at large. It is obvious to both Ann and I, "perfection" would preclude sin, evil and karma and obviate the need for such but how do you convince people, with programs of this already installed in their minds, to accept the opposite? Most everyone would rather go around finding fault, evil and sin in others rather than concentrating on "fixing" themselves and unlocking their inherent Divine selves.

Yet, even James had believed until recently, Karma was an unavoidable consequence of living on Planet Earth! James had an epiphany about one day as he cogitated this idea and shared it with Ann, "You know Ann, as much as we have learned about Karma from Buddhism, Kriya Kundalini Yoga and Hinduism, I have the strongest feeling we really do not understand this concept and it is in fact possible to get off the proverbial "Wheel of Karma" that Buddhist's and Hindu's constantly mention. I mean, I was already leaning that way but after visiting those amazing ancient trees in the Kings Canyon Wilderness area and the millennia's old trees at The General Grant Redwood Grove, I know these trees know more about this than the Buddhists, Hindus, Kabbalists, Gnostic Christians, Christian Scientists or anybody else!. At its essence within the purview of physics, Karma basically boils down to concept, for every action there is an equal and opposite reaction. And within this construct, it could mean you will get the results of actions immediately and there will not necessarily be a residual affect to this! **So Karma does not linger like an albatross around your neck, as Hinduism and Buddhism have taught, unless you believe such!** You really do not need Jesus to "save you from your sins," as if someone other than yourself could do this anyway! I guess the only way to explain this to the hoards of people who will resist this, is to go back to the explanation of our acts within the purview of Physics."

James continued, "Despite the fact there might be good intentions involved in getting people to be aware of their karma, the good and bad actions that affect other people, people literally get trapped in the Karma Dogma. It becomes counterproductive, for at least some people who already live their lives at a high level, people who do the right and best things with the highest intentions, to the highest of their ability. Furthermore, **believing we are being constantly negatively affected by our Karma literally creates more of the same in the subconscious/unconscious mind!** Of this I am very sure and, ha-ha, so are the ancient trees!"

Rather amused by James "annihilating the box," once again, Ann replied, "Although I never considered what you shared, exactly in the way you shared it, Mr. Smarty Pants, your way of framing this makes a lot of sense, even though it goes against everything believed on Planet Earth. Interesting enough, the concept of Karma does not really have a place in the higher realms of Heaven, my abode now, because everyone already knows they are Divine, they are perfect, as per *Aleph Kaf Aleph*, which of course, changes the whole game!"

Finding himself somewhat assured by Ann's remarks, James responded, "Whew, I thought I might be completely in Looneysville with my highly unorthodox ideas on karma and it seems my pants might still be smart... we will see, *se la vie*! I am not implying we should not live good and virtuous lives and help our fellowman; I am just saying people can be unduly trapped in their Karma by their obsession with such. And for you and I, Ann, we already have that service to humanity, mentality. But this Hindu/Buddhist belief that you need to live at least a couple thousand lifetimes to get of The Wheel of Karma, is patently untrue and my friends, the ancient trees I communicate with, have shown and told me as much! I have already reprogrammed my mind to my ideas so I have a real chance of pulling off this immortality gig! I have nothing against wheels, just those that have karma attached to them and don't want any karma holding me back, like an anchor, since my natural composition and impetus is to be only Divine.

"Well certainly the Hindu and Buddhist churches get more revenue from people who keep reincarnating back into their religion, so they have no motivation to change their 'false doctrines." And the Christian and Moslem churches are not going to give up the sin/evil syndrome because they get money from their parishioners, who want to be saved through their ceremonies! Everything seems to break down to monetary issues and the need for a constant stream of revenue from sinners. I could name names of the worst offending churches but will not, ha-ha, since you already know what I will say.

Laughingly, James replied, "Please remember, Ann, what I am about to say does not come from my own lips, but I know you are referring to the Catholic Church, which many people have named a criminal enterprise! There is ample proof of this but once again, do not ascribe these ideas to me, please, ha-ha! There are enough people already pissed off at me since the truth is a very sharp sword that cuts with precision!

Both James and Ann laughed hysterically for several minutes about James' statements! To which James exclaimed, "Let me know if my ass starts falling off, Ann, from my unbridled laughing."

"It appears your ass is still intact for the present time, anyway, ha-ha!"

CHAPTER ELEVEN

Starting To Enter Heaven And Leaving
The Wheel Of Karma Behind
What's So Hard About This?
Déjà Vu –
We Have All Done This And Been There

———— ✦ ————

THE CURIOUS THING about Karma, which is so completely misunderstood and misperceived is... every time your life ends on Earth, your Karma here is left behind on Earth, even though it might be carried along in you DNA, as recorded data! So the question which still confronted James was, "Can you leave your Karma behind, immediately through the process of death, as we have all done before; or whether the physics aspect of Karma, for every action there is an equal and opposite reaction, would negate any long term effects of Karma, since there is an unavoidable cleansing of the negative karma, likewise, as long as your acts toward others, were at worst, neutral/non detrimental; or whether you are inextricably trapped in your karma for at least 2000 life times?

As James cogitated on this dilemma he concluded, "I believe I have left or have significantly left the Wheel of Karma behind, in this lifetime, as I live by the template of doing no harm to anyone and I am ready to immortalize my body in the here and now of this incarnation! But how can I prove this to myself, irrespective of what others believe? I guess that comes from how smoothly my life manifests. If things are flowing, I am sure I am growing and ready to leave behind my old baggage. Thus, I can enter a state of Heaven on Earth and enter Soruba Samadhi, provided I keep raising the Prana/Chi/God-life force in my body through Kriya Kundalini Pranayam, Sun Gazing, things like Tulsi Basil and hot peppers, the Tai Chi "Standing Meditation," Sanskrit mantra recitation and reciting *The 72 Names of God* from *Exodus* of *The Torah*. These things create an alchemical reaction, The Intelligent Cosmic Vibration, a reflection/refraction of the so called physical body, culminating in a transfiguration of the form operating only as energy and with no vestiges of "matter" and its properties of "dense energy." All those things I am a doing so big things must be a brewing! As we become happy, as a bean, we can begin to wean ourselves from the constrictions of the controllers on Earth and destroy their totalitarian schemes, part of which is trapping or imprisoning us in some state of physical deterioration! This, unfortunately, leaves us subject to the subtle manipulation of government, religions, and corporations.

Absorbing all of this Ann eagerly chimed in, "I am surprised you have not mentioned Dr. Paul Foster Case's book, *The Esoteric Keys of Alchemy*, Mr. Smarty Pants, and Case's organization, Builders of the Adytum (BOTA). Neither did you mention Paracelsus. These are two of the most famous Alchemists, the first from modern times and the later from ancient times. Certainly the elements of water, fire and Mercury have transformative powers to unleash a transfiguration of the human body into a state of immortality!"

"I knew I could count on you to put my feet in the fire, Ann, and yet I was just about to get to Dr. Case! You know he is one of my very few heroes and yet even *The Esoteric Keys of Alchemy* says the Alchemical process of immortalizing the body cannot be specifically delineated and only explained in general terms. Near the end of the Alchemical transformation, Case says it is up to us to uncover the last things that free us from a physical body. For sure, the water element is indispensible for this and probably that is why I like to surf. As for the fire, well, I am a Scorpio and the third stage of Scorpio is to become immersed and consumed in the fire and from the ashes of the fire, the Phoenix, the immortal bird, manifests.

So luckily for me, my astrology is giving me a boost and advantage to me pulling off the alchemical immortality!

Ha! How many people have tried to burn you, Mr. Smarty Pants, yet in that they fail, ha-ha! But remember, as Dr. Case said in *Esoteric Keys of Astrology,* God is the "primal force" and we are inextricably tied to that, like a seed is to its source tree. This would relate to the Élan Vitale, the vital life force, which is the same as The Intelligent Cosmic Vibration from *The Bhagavad Gita!* Dr. Case recommends Yoga Practice, meditation and visualization to prepare the mind for alchemical immortality/transfiguration! Yet he also recommends eating "true foods" which are probably unprocessed foods, and controlling how much we eat. He also talks about sexual moderation and the importance of proper kidney elimination. Perhaps most importantly, he discusses removing anything that prevents us absorbing "… the light of the life power."

James replied after considering Ann's counsel, "Well, certainly we have talked about the power of light (Agna) and the factor of fire (Yagna), of which Dr. Case was most versed in. And certainly the Sanskrit mantras anchor and amplify the Agna and Yagna in us, especially the primal sound, "Aum/Om", *The Gayatri Mantra* and the *Maha Mrityunjaya Mantra*. Probably not coincidentally, the latter two mantras are salutations to the Sun and are known for their power in protecting people and their primal force, Intelligent Cosmic Vibration. Aspects of this directly **relate to immortalizing our bodies and as we realize as God is indestructible, we must inevitably be so ourselves!"**

Ann found herself kind of amazed, and noting to James it is rather hard to amaze an Angel, stated, "Once again, Mr. Smarty Pants, your "box-less thinking" has saved the day and your body too, ha-ha, Happy Halloween! What I mean is it will also "save" your body from the normally accepted ravages of Planet Earth."

"Well, my Ms. Smarty Pants, you set up the concepts that allowed me to get to these realizations… that were instrumental in visualizing what we or I need to do for the indestructible body. And you know what, Ann, we all deserve such if we so wish it, irrespective of the religious authorities that tell us otherwise, that we have to die to find our salvation and immortality and the businesses that profit from our slowly, "slip sliding away" into a state of bodily death, namely doctors, hospitals and the pharmaceutical companies! *Se la vie, mon ami!* Our time is now, as it were! I am basking in the immortalizing energies of the Sun, like the Walrus, Koo Koo Ka Choo.

CHAPTER TWELVE

So We Need To Delve Into Whether We
Are Living In a "Time Machine
Is The Transcendence Of Time Another
Way To Create The Body Immortal?

———— ⚜ ————

IN CONTINUING AN active quest to immortalize his body, James thoughts got stuck on a particular topic. *Imagine if there were no time! Would that stop the aging process?* The social psychologist, Dr. Ellen Langers, showed results in her Harvard study that indicate such. I am certainly well aware of this study and the implications thereof, which revealed when people *live in an environment from a time when they were younger, their bodies literally start reversing the aging process! This is accomplished by tricking the mind into believing the body is getting younger! So what is really more important, age and time, themselves, or how the brain-mind, our personal-personal computer, actually view age and time?"*

Feeling uncomfortable being relegated to nothing more than his own thoughts, James was compelled to speak aloud to whomever might want to listen! "Interestingly enough, I am already transcending the bounds of time when I go into the deep meditation, known as Kriya Kundalini Pranayam and Samadhi! The extremely extended breathing regimen in Pranayam, due to inhaling through the nostrils into the diaphragm first and then pulling the breath fully into the lungs, makes it possible to extend the exhale twice as long as the inhale cycle! This doubly long exhale is facilitated by mudras, which are things done with the tongue and the eyes, making such a breath possible. Without these mudras, it is very difficult, if not impossible, to accomplish the extended Pranayam breath!"

"Beyond this, as it were, the Pranayam breath naturally leads to the breathless state of Samadhi, in experienced practitioners, thereof, after which said practitioner of Pranayam can extend each breathing cycle to at least twenty-five to thirty seconds and more. For me, accomplishing the forty-second breathing cycle is so liberating I transcend periods of time during my meditation involving this. The real transcending of time, however, manifests in the breathless state of Samadhi, when the heart stops beating and the blood ceases circulating. Of course, this has nothing to do with holding one's breath but rather entering a higher dimension of consciousness. Not only is the brain not damaged, even after doing this for several hours, all the senses are heightened as Samadhi produces brainwaves in the Theta and even upper Delta range!"

One would question whether it is these deeper brainwaves that put us in a higher dimension; that account for the transcendence of time in a kind of time warp. It would seem to be what is going down, the higher the dimension we access... the less time seems to be relevant. So whether there is a connection between the more complex geometric forms in these higher dimensions and the process of suspending time that is the real question.

With this in mind, James noted, "There is the numeral value of the word "time" and it is 47 with the inverse being 74. Also, the inverse of time happens to be "emit" or to put forth, so 47 equates to Abraham and Brahmin, both holy names in Judaism and Hinduism. Jesus and Lucifer (an Angel of light) equates to 74 and Christ equals 47. The atomic number of Silver is 47 and the atomic weight of titanium is likewise 47; 74 connotes both light and darkness, is the atomic number of tungsten and is an Angel Number, so you should relate to that, Ann!

"So the key or keys to transcending time and its purported effects may lie in using the light of Lucifer and Jesus, who was reported to come to Earth in a Merkabah, body of light, in *The Secrets of Sion,* which is about the Gnostic Christian texts. So what do we know that enhances the light and fire? Could it be the Agna and Yagna, found in the Intelligent Cosmic Vibration? And what do we know, Ann that fosters those properties? Could it be Kriya Kundalini Pranayam and the Tai Chi Standing Meditation? Could it be the Sanskrit Mantras of Aum, Gayatri and Mahamrityonjaya?

Ann, with a real fervor, replied, Well, Mr. Smarty Pants, definitely Pranayam is a breath beyond panting, as it were! Certainly there are four distinct seasonal cycles on Earth but they do not have to be inextricably intertwined with time. More likely, that is just how we have chosen to experience such. Also, the fact we can go forward or backward in time, through remote viewing, could well indicate there is no "real time," as we have accepted! Additionally, there are quantum physicists who believe the past, present and future all occur concurrently. "

"So if they have the properties of concurrence, this indicates there is no real passing of time, to age us and lead us to our demise. The reason I share these things, James of the Smart Pants, because in the ninth dimension of heaven, wherein I reside, this is exactly what occurs. Good luck convincing the humans on Earth of this, yet it is as it is here! And anyway, you already know this because of your ability to move your consciousness into my dimension."

"Certainly, the light factors you mentioned, Pranayam, the Tai Chi Standing Mediation, and the Sanskrit Mantras, infuse the body with the Agna and Yagna of the Intelligent Cosmic Vibration. In with this perspective, that there is an intense manifestation of light here in the ninth dimension of heaven, and we do not measure and thus are unaffected by the passage of time! But does time really pass? Is there something or some force making it "move" or "transit"? I have detected no force or mechanism to provide the impetus for this where I am, nor have you, James, where you are."

"James, you are certainly a persistent and adventurous "little bugga!"

James laughingly replied, "Don't you remember in *That Mysterious Flow*, by Paul Davies in *Scientific American,* Sept. 2002, where he discussed how there is no special now and the past and present are basically one thing with the now. So this "little bugga" has been doing his homework. "If you try to get your hands on time, it is slipping through your hands," reveals Julian Barbour. Einstein was depicting time as "relative" in his "Theory of Relativity;" Sir Isaac Newton saw time "as basically a river," but does that river have elements that make us inextricably age? **In fact there is no such component of inherent aging yet we have in fact been programmed through our schools and religions this is so!** Thus we need to deprogram such idiocy from our brain/mind as per Dr. Newton's and my book, *A Map to Healing and Your Essential Divinity Through Theta Consciousness* or some other modality like NLP. "

"Also, *In the Path of the Phoenix*, Robert Coon talks about how gratitude will open our heart and set us on a path to immortality and the grand plan this is a part of! This gratitude factor is a lubricant and catalyst that inextricably puts us into an alignment with our Creator and this creates "the magic" that allows this process of transfiguration. I am feeling what he is saying is related to *Ayin Nun Vav*, which is appreciation that equates to gratitude. "

Ann rejoined in what had gotten to be a rather natural banter,

"Well, James of the Smarty Pants, you seem to have figured out how we age and why we do not need to. We could go sideways and say also, we do not need to be sick and we do not have to be sick unless our thoughts are "sick", likewise, as is well explained in *A Map to Healing and Your Essential Divinity Through Theta Consciousness*. So we have been programmed into believing in sickness and death and inevitably manifest such in our lives through our thoughts and emotions, as per *Science and Health with Key to the Scriptures* and *You Can Heal Your Life*. Certainly, the concept of time aging us should be deader than a doornail! And even if time does exists, if we believe it does not exist, we do not have to be affected by the ravages of time, because they become non-operational in our lives and thus irrelevant, since our brain or mind no longer identifies with such! When this gratitude happens is when the *eternal us* starts to be revealed."

"Tangentially related to this, Dr. Lothar Schaffer, *In Search of Divine Purpose*, relates there is unlimited empty space in the Quantum Field, just waiting for us to come along and partake in such. Extending this idea, why would there not be unlimited time in this same quantum field? And with said unlimited time, **it would create a field of timelessness,** and there would be no way to relate to the passing of unlimited time and **the long held belief of the natural deterioration of the human body would become virtually irrelevant!**"

So the night of James' conversation with Ann, during his sojourns in parallel Earth dimensions and the higher dimensions beyond this, which most people would describe as the dream state, James saw what would be happening to him during the process of the impending immortalizing of his body. In these multiple places, of which James was familiar and comfortable, to wit, he saw himself going into Soruba (permanent) Samadhi, after performing 30 minutes of Kriya Kundalini Pranayam, the very extended breathing meditation he had mastered and performed every day.

As he entered the breathless state of Soruba Samadhi, James activated a Kundalini awakening from all of the Prana/Chi/God-life force. Fortunately for James, he had experienced a Kundalini Awakening multiple times in the past. This was fortunate in that a full force Kundalini Awakening is an intense and disorienting experience! So much Prana is pouring into the body, it feels like your face is burning up with an almost unbearable heat sensation. Likewise, there is tremendous energy running up and down the spine, from the root chakra, in the sexual region, up into the crown chakra, at the top of the head. All of this, as intense as it is, is less in scope in comparison to being thrown into the fifth and sixth dimensions, where things become less dense matter and things are not really solid and everything has an auric energy field around it.

Yet, this is all tolerable since consciousness is shifted into a state of bliss and a deeper connection to The Creator than anyone would have thought is possible. James' curiosity was very piqued as he pondered, *I wonder if and when this state of Soruba Samadhi will be happening in my life? I know when I am in a deep Pranayam meditation I am in state of somewhat transcending time. When I transit into a temporary state of Samadhi, I am pretty much in a state of timelessness. It will be most interesting to see what will happen in my life on the frontier of consciousness, immortality!*

CHAPTER THIRTEEN

Finally, Living In An Immortalized Body,
Happy As A Bean,
And Weaning Ourselves From The
Constrictions of the Controllers On
Earth!
How Do We Create Heaven On Earth, As
Per Aleph Kaf Aleph?

———— ·ᴥ· ————

JAMES FELT THINGS were moving along with enough proof and direction that the quest to immortalize his body was not the deluded notions of a fool. And if such were even considered the rantings of a fool, such fool was in the vein of *The Tarot*, a person who would tread fearless where others dare not to go! Certainly, James had many signs his body was regenerating and was now functioning at about the age of a forty year old man, even though he was sixty-nine years old!

One morning, upon awakening from his dimensional sojourns (dreams), completing his Pranayama meditation, and going into the naturally following Samadhi, James did in fact go into Soruba Samadhi in conjunction with a Kundalini Awakening, and he made a so-called impossible shift to an immortalized body. *Considering all my trepidation about this event,* James opined, *this feels so good and balancing, as opposed to my first Kundalini Awakening! All my energies are balanced, and my body is in a state of energy, as opposed to dense matter. All my aches and pains and spinal* *problems have vanished. My psychic abilities are even more well-honed than before. More importantly, I feel the constant presence of God's love and I must say it exceeds the best aspects of human love! While everyone else, including my son and my fiancé, thought I was looneysville, only you Ann, in discarnate form, knew this was possible! I knew I could make the impossible possible, as per Vav Vav Lamed, and I constantly focused my thoughts on this, since in the end, **nothing is impossible**!*

Yet there are those sight perceptual differences in things, like objects no longer being completely solid, like how things and people seem to be wavy, non completely solid forms, James observed. "Yes, I have seen this after a localized, segmented Kundalini awakening but that was temporary in nature. Now, I will simply have to learn to adjust to this effect of being/living in the fifth dimension and beyond. I will simply have to approach things from the perspective of *Resh Hey Ayin*, the 39th Name of God, meaning, finding the good in the bad. I am working myself toward not seeing "bad" anywhere, and only perceiving "good".

As James considered all of this the more he realized, *I guess I am going have to get used to seeing through people's clothes and bodies. Hopefully, a level of detachment will allow to neither get excited or not excited about my new viewing of things. Maybe I will become a famous psychic healer and put my hand into people's bodies and remove tumors and such. Probably I will learn to surf on the ocean without a surfboard, ha-ha! There are definitely "new settings" on my psychic abilities. Maybe I can promote myself as world famous psychic, and beyond-o... who knows more than humanly possible.*

"We will see, *se la vie*, but actually there are more important things into which to direct my energy, the real reason why I was so fanatically focused on immortalizing my body! For sure, there is such a surreal feel to the way I am experiencing things now."

It is difficult for me to prove this, but I feel the broad based approach I used in this quest for immortality was responsible for me getting off "The Wheel of Karma" and establishing a body of light, a Merkabah, infused with the Yagna and Agna of the Prana and the

Intelligent Cosmic Vibration. Certainly, there is already clear evidence that using Kriya Kundalini Pranayam to go into Samadhi and then a continual Samadhi, Soruba Samadhi. Yet the alchemical catalyst factors of the Sanskrit mantras, *The 72 Names of God*, The *Tai Chi Standing Meditation*, as well as ingesting and absorbing Ormus, and the Habanero Pepper tincture, and using the ASEA water, was a definite factor in my transformation from matter to spirit, light, and energy! My intuition supports this conclusion, likewise.

James was so focused on creating Heaven on Earth after he attained Soruba Samadhi, he really did not have time to bask in his accomplishment, otherwise viewed as his desired transfiguration or transformation! Remembering what Ann had said the day before, James, considering all of this then explained, "Certainly we can be weaned from the many myths of the controllers on Earth, whose vested interests that make money **from** our purported frailty, have foisted upon us! Let doornails be dead as they should, and let us move forward. Let us realize the concept of *Resh Hey Ayin*, the 39th Name of God from *Exodus* in *The Torah*, which means finding the good in the bad."

Continuing his communication with Ann, James continued, "I have actually thought a lot about this name and am convinced there is no bad or evil, unless we create or allow such in our lives! This bad-ness or evil can never spontaneously manifest themselves into our lives just out of the blue, even though others have tried to teach us the opposite! Let us take the attitude of The Fool, from *The Tarot,* and move forward fearlessly into our Divine inheritance and our right to be immortal!

Delighted, James heard Ann chime in, "Insightful you are, Master Yoda! So a Jedi you want to be?"

Bordering on mania, James' laughter echoed from the walls. "So a Jedi I must already be... and a Fool to wit, but the good kind of Fool, the propitious Fool! But either way, I want to be free from the dysfunctional thoughts that have crippled us as a people on Earth. Immortality of our existing bodies, we have revealed as a real possibility—and even more so, our right and beyond that—an actuality! There will be myriad people, hopefully a tidal wave of them, who realize they can live forever, as they so choose! Now we must use the wisdom and valuable experiences of what will be the immortalized Elders and create Heaven on Earth. Despite the naysayers who claim things are too screwed up to save or change, *ah, contraire!* it just ignores the underlying perfection of things, easily observable on the atomic level of existence, and as per the Seventh Name of God, *Aleph Kaf Aleph*, which is restoring things to their perfect state!

Ann contributed to the conversation by asking James another question, "Are you really sure about that, Master Yoda? Well, actually I know you are, but how are you going to sell the truisms we have uncovered? Would you like some angelic help?

James replied with absolute certainty, "In fact, I can use all the help I can get, angelic and otherwise—and who can more powerfully focus energy than an angel, huh? We are swimming against the clichéd surge of a tidal wave, in a manner of speaking!

Ann responded, "Duh, to the angelic force, but then again I am prejudiced in my perspectives! But if we are all connected to the Light/God, as per the 59th Name of God, *Hey Resh Chet*, we are just as connected to each other through this light, and the commensurate love attached thereto, really inseparable in a non-dualistic sense. That is precisely how you and I can communicate, Ann... cross dimensionally! This connecting light is also how we link our hearts together, to melt away the greed and hoarding and begin really to share resources!!

James rejoined, "Well, we know we do not have to deteriorate now nor does our planet and the civilizations thereon. But before I get to the civilization part, I just wanted to add some things I dug up on the Internet, which are germane to us personally, and then I will try to make the big leap and apply this to rebuilding our planet!"

"So I think we talked about this previously, but in the Shamatha Project, led by Fahri Saatcioglu at the University of Oslo, they found intensive meditators had thirty percent longer telomere strands in their DNA. And that, Mr. Smarty Pants knows, leads to better health and extended life spans! So what if this applied to our

Earth, that it too has DNA and telomere strands, which are either enhanced or diminished according to the thoughts and emotions of its inhabitants! That is *usmundo*, essentially us, Ann... the whole of humanity!

Excitedly, James continued, "This same study project found Yoga Asanas deep Yogic breathing, via Sudarshan Kriya yoga and meditation, elicit a relaxation response that has a long term affect on gene expression, and a lengthening of the telomere strands that also manifest as a strengthening of our immune systems! Added to this, it was discovered in this project that nature walks and music driven meditation change 38 genes. Once more we have a telomere lengthening affect occurring, so if the World's people get control of their thoughts through meditation, imagine Earth healing and becoming a sort of heaven where things operate in a higher dimension. Is this not what happens when we meditate? Imagine that, Ann?"

What if the electro magnetic energy ley lines were our Earth DNA strands? What if the cities connected to these lines were the telomere strands, and what if the people of the city were the telomerase enzyme that make the telomere longer and make the city healthier, more livable?

Ann summarily responded to James, "That would be most amazing... and some then!"

"That is not all, Ann," James replied. "Still other studies by researchers Jan Sev Singh and Sat Bir Singh Khalsa, PhD., at the Benson-Henry Institute for Mind-Body Medicine at the Massachusetts General Hospital, Harvard Medical School, reveal long term practitioners of meditation or yoga, and even novices, who had only been meditating for eight weeks, significant alterations in cellular metabolism, oxidative phosphorylation, generation of reactive oxygen and response to additive stress... that may counteract cellular damage related to psychological stress. This, again, is related to DNA telomerase enzymes being produced that in turn, lengthen the DNA telomere strands. I think we can be confident, Ann, what this reveals, is bringing more Prana into the human body corrects imperfections therein! Would not the same

101

thing happen to the Earth, likewise—as we perfect ourselves—we perfect our Earth Mother?

Talking more to himself, in trying to sort things out, than communicating with Ann, James carried on... "The same things were found in a succeeding study done by doctors Helen Lavretsky and Dharma Singh Khalsa at the UCLA Alzheimer's Research and Prevention Foundation, where quantified daily meditation lead to improved mental and cognitive functioning and reduced stress when combined with Kirtan Kriya meditation. Also revealed was increased telomere activity and maintenance! Another study by a Dr. Benson showed changes in expression of genes with energy metabolism, mitochondrial function, insulin secretion and telomere maintenance, and additional reduced expression of genes related to inflammatory response and stress related issues! So the theme of our leaving a personal imprint on Earth DNA from our level of stress and health, and our resulting DNA, appears again! Again and again and again... you can see the evidence of optimizing our own DNA leads to an optimization of Earth DNA to a Golden Age and Heaven on Earth!"

Ann added her input, "I know that makes you happy beyond belief, Mr. Smarty, and it is so cool-mundo and auspicious for Earth, as well as *usmundo... .all of us*! Literally, these are all meditations you do, and actually much more and deeper, so you must be cooler than an iceberg or a glacier! So now I guess you are going to elaborate on how this relates to our civilization and societies on Earth, huh?

James laughingly replied, "Well in a sense I already have and you are definitely right on that, my Ms. Smarty, ha-ha! Yet I am thinking, and you certainly know this, how much more powerful the Kriya Kundalini Yoga Pranayam Meditation is than Kundalini Yoga and Kirtan Kriya and Sudarshan Kriya. Of this, we are both certain and yet I cannot find studies to verify what we **know** as a certainty!

Ann, after contemplating all of James' information, replied in her usual banter, "Right-e-o, Mr. Smarty... Kriya Kundalini Pranayam **is** the singular most cutting edge breathing meditation and the most transforming thing anyone can do from any of the many of the traditions you and I studied and that includes almost everything, ha-ha! That there is proof these lesser meditations are stimulating telomerase enzymes and lengthening the DNA, means the extremely extended breathing cadence of Pranayam causes the transformation in a vastly magnified manner! "

In a more serious approach James then responded, "Yes, for you and I, but more importantly me, since you are already are in the ninth dimension of Heaven, and inherently immortalized; we have everything we need to immortalize the human body." The bigger question remains, how, then, do we get the Earth's DNA maximized beyond controlling our thoughts and emotions, via meditation, so as to catalyze things into the Seventh Name of God, *Aleph Kaf Aleph* and restore Earth to its perfect state. Certainly, Dr. Newton and I definitely shared how this can happen as related to how to reconstruct our economy and banking/monetary systems on Earth, in the last three or four chapters of the book, *Beyond the Mists of Time: When Trees Ruled the Earth*, but we never considered addressing the Earth's DNA!

Musing over the concepts James addressed, Ann suddenly exclaimed, "Wow, Mr. Smarty, you have decided to take a large, bite, a rather huge chunk on this issue haven't you? Actually, now that I think about it... actually, a humongous one! I have never known anyone even have the audacity to discuss the Earth's DNA! But in fact it must have one since everything seems to be created from computer codes, as the physicist, Dr. Hubert Yockey discusses, re humans, in *Information Theory, Evolution and the Origin of Life*. In the case of humans, it is a binary pairs computer code. For the Anunaki, who inhabited ancient Sumer, there is evidence from their DNA, which indicated a twelve strand DNA''

James returned to the conversation, stating, It really does not matter whether the Earth's DNA is a binary pair, two strand, or a twelve strand, since there are a huge number of combinations with only binary pairs. So if our human DNA is affected by meditation, Sanskrit mantras, including "*Aum, The Gayatri Mantra, and the Maha Mrityunjaya Mantra* and *The 72 Names* of God, why would our own Earth not be affected by the same things, as per *The Emerald Tablets of Hermes Trismegustis*, where that which is **above** is affected by that which is **below** and vice versa. I think this is the last ingredient Dr. Newton and I were looking for to create the New Heaven on Earth in *Beyond the Mist of Time: When Trees Ruled the Earth*!

Feeling amazed, Ann replied, "I have no idea how you figured this out, Mr. Smarty, as it is difficult even to ascertain this from the highest realms of Heaven!"

To which James replied, "We both know there is no I... or me... or you in how this came to about! A lot of it was inspired by Dr. Hurtak's book, *The Keys of Enoch*" and Dr. Yockey's book, *Information Theory, Evolution and the Origin of Life*. Let's just say these concepts, as well as accessing The *Akashic Records* as described in *The Vedas* and *Celestial Hearing* as described in Patanjali's, *The Yoga Sutras,* were instrumental into bringing this information forth! When the requisite information is not available on Earth, you have to go otherworldly, as I described, getting information from the skies (Akashic) and auditory, telepathic, or clairaudience (Celestial Hearing)."

There was no stopping the message delivered by James, "So yes, Ann, we need to eliminate corporations and their proclivity to hoarding and monopolizing of resources! Just as we need to eliminate the present economic system of private banking and vapor currencies with no inherent value. Let's not forget we need to make it so no one can possess more than they can use, to eliminate the virulent disease of greed! And even more, we need to discard the religions that trap us in their boxes of hell, evil and sin, so we might ultimately express our inherently Divine selves as we were originally and fundamentally created."

"Just think about it, Ann, if we do this from the inside out, using the deep meditation techniques, especially Pranayam and the Sanskrit Mantras, especially Aum, Gayatri, and Mahamrityunjaya and The 72 Names of God, the Earth can make that transformation. And that conversion will come from people using the above things to bring themselves into a state of immortality. It can also come from general meditation, but the specific things just mentioned are like an Autobahn to the process... making it happen faster! All these things open the Pineal Gland, which is like a cosmic antenna into the dimensions of the Divine and *Aleph Kaf Aleph...* to restore things to their perfect state! This is like coming in through the back door since there will be massive resistance by the global elite and the CEO's to the even distribution of things. Somehow, these higher ups have concluded they are more important than the rest of us and entitled to obscene and unnecessary amount of wealth and possessions. The greed these people harbor is the most virulent disease (lack of ease) on planet Earth!"

James felt his voice raise in the passion of his words, "Certainly, there is enough money and resources on Earth for everyone to share in the bounty! The true injustice of this is evident in someone like the Dunkin Donuts CEO making almost $4,900 an hour and then proclaiming he cannot afford to pay his employees a fifteen dollar an hour minimum wage. To call this man an insensitive and ignorant prick would be an understatement! So we have a big challenge here we can overcome with *Vav Vav Lamed* — and make the impossible possible!" **We can make it so the wayward souls, the greedy ones, will have no choice but to open their hearts and share their bounty, if enough of us begin repeating and focusing on Vav Vav Lamed.** This sounds too easy yet the energy behind our sacred Hebrew names have **power and effect.**

"This makes me even more pumped to manifest the immortal Earth, with liberty and justice and bounty for all! Then I and my fellow immortals, the Enlightened Elders, can share and enact our wisdom in a manner where everyone truly shares in the wealth and we can jettison the global elite, Illuminati and related ilk, and their pernicious bankers to the second dimension, where they belong! Remember, Ann, how strongly Dr. Newton and I talked about this extensively in our book, *"Beyond the Mists of Time: When Trees Ruled the Earth?* We were equally passionate then to plant thee seeds to change the operating systems on Earth to a Zeitgeist... to thrive by sharing the wealth mentality!"

Hardly stopping to take a breath, James unceasing challenged life's events, "Earth is moving to at worst, the fourth dimension, anyway. Thus this will no longer be an Earth for those who cannot learn to share and do not want to align with this "program"! Additionally, this will help prepare the way for the success of Dan Winter's, "Earth Heartbeat Project", wherein the resonance field of the linked hearts will dispense the love and compassion necessary to create Heaven on Earth. Imagine all the light that will be released when hearts join together. We will probably leave the fourth dimension behind and begin moving into the fifth range!

Ann, absorbing all of this could only say, "Wow!"

James, attempting to be a bit more light-hearted sarcastically replied, "Bow-wow! Even my dog, Bink, gets this idea, so it is time for us humans to get it, likewise! If I look at *The 72 Names of God*, I know this is doable; manifest-table (a table full of bounty and riches). I know *Hey Resh Chet* connects us to the light/God; *Mem Nun Daled* allows me to overcome my fears, which allows me to make the impossible possible as per *Vav Vav Lamed*, which then removes obstacles as per *Yod Chet Vav*. This then allows us to fix our past and create our happiness via *Vav Hey Vav*, which serves to boost the energy that is essential to become immortal, as per *Yod Lamed Yod*. Taking it further, we can then manifest a state of miracles, as per *Samesh Yod Tet!* So... Ann, when we are in this state of miracles, I believe anything is possible and achievable for us. Therefore, as a certainty, *Ayin Resh Yod*, we can pull off this gig of immortality, certain and most true!"

His voice softened considerably as James delivered the next statement, "Well actually you **have** pulled it off, Ann, and the illusion of time is waiting for me to do so likewise! I am waiting on pins and needles for it to manifest."

He felt no need to use his voice, as James transferred his thoughts to Ann, *I have to believe by overcoming our fears, we can do the impossible; as obstacles are removed, which allows us to fix ourselves and create a state of happiness for ourselves, we then boost our energy sufficiently to create miracles. And one of these miracles is Hey Hey Ayin, unconditional love smothering planet Earth!*

Soft enough for the voice of an Angel, James said, "¡*Hasta luego, mon amour*, Ann, of the Angelic Pants!

About the Author

Dr. Robert J. Newton has lived his life much in the manner he writes... with a quest to surround himself with the highest level knowledge in the myriad areas that ensure we live rich, full lives. His education has been extensive, ranging from Speech and English at Cal State Fullerton, to a Juris Doctorate from American College of Law, and many certifications in alternative healing. He formalized his career in Naturopathic Medicine as a graduate of Clayton School of Natural Healing.

Newton has lived to serve others; operating an award-winning landscape and design company for many years, as a Christian Science healer for two decades, and more recently as an author, speaker and life and relationship coach. Yoga, Metaphysics, Spiritual Sciences, Natural Healing, World Religions, Ancient Hermetic teachings... this philosopher and champion for the world has tapped into the roots of spirituality, sexuality, life and love—all with the purpose to enlighten those with a common desire to utilize multiple methods and strategies to approach life more effectively, creatively, radiantly and with great abundance.

Today, Dr. Newton lives his life looking forward... honoring the love and the beliefs he shared with his wife, and writing more novels to plant a "What if" seed in the minds of his readers.

Glossary of Terms

If you are a student of the area of life and science about which Dr. Newton writes, you will be most comfortable with these words; however, in respect for all readers, the following glossary of terms is intended to enrich your understanding of the book. You may want to study the terms and maybe even print them out so you will have a ready reference to define some words with which you may be unfamiliar.

Agna: This is light associated with Prana and "The Intelligent Cosmic Vibration." It is part and parcel with Yagna cymatic(s): Vibrations such as found in vowel sounds, especially in Sanskrit Mantras and the Hebrew "72 Names of God," from "Exodus" 14: 19-21 in The Torah.

Alpha brainwave: This is a moderately relaxing and creative brainwave, where sports performance can be enhanced, also. It is the first altered state of consciousness/awareness you "enter" when doing Yoga, Meditation, Sanskrit mantras and the Hebrew "72 Names of God." It occurs in the hertz range of 7-13 or 14 hz.

Aum: In India and the Orient, this is considered the primal, originating sound of creation that brings things into manifestation. It is a Sanskrit word and mantra (rosary) with extremely active vowel sounds and there is a picture in the body of this book which shows the geometric waveforms created when this word is vocalized. This sound, applied to a human body, puts the body in a higher form of energy, Prana, Chi, God life-force and shift the mind into the higher functioning, more relaxed, more creative brainwaves of Alpha, Theta and Delta

Beta brainwave: This is considered a normal brainwave in the range of 13-14 hertz and above. Lots of stress and low productivity is often experience in this "low functioning" brainwave

Breathairianism: The discipline of living without the eating of food and in some cases, without drink. Some Breatharians take juice for nutrient, and almost all do sun gazing and sun bathing, since they fill the body with the electrical and light nutrients, known as Prana/Chi/God life force. Also many such practitioners perform Kriya Kundalini Pranayam or Kundalini Yoga for body nitrification. There is a documentary, *In the Beginning There was Light,* which explains and portrays Breathairianism.

Chi: Electromagnetic energy from Source/God/Creator that can make physical alternation in the physical body and corresponding brain wave alternation into the Alpha-Theta-Delta range

Delta brainwaves: A brainwave at 4 Hertz and below. This usually is experienced in sleep and the so-called "dream state". It is possible to experience this during Samadhi in a state of consciousness and in other very deep meditations after a long duration of meditating.

Gayatri Mantra: A Sanskrit mantra/prayer to the Sun/God and the many Sanskrit vowels in this mantra are very atomically active, meaning they have an altering and calming yet energizing effect on the human body, as well as altering human brainwaves into the alpha-theta-delta range. The vibrations from this mantra create the Shri Yantra (Mandala)

God life force: The same as Chi.

Intelligent Cosmic Vibration: Comprised of Prana and vowel cymatic/vibrations as found in Sanskrit mantras.

Kinesiology muscle testing: A method to ascertain the value and validity of something for an individual person. It involves either using the muscle of the arm or of the fingers, asking a series of yes and no answers. Refer to Chapter Three of A Map to Healing and Your Essential Divinity Through Theta Consciousness for diagrams and directions on how to do this.

Kriya Asanas: A choreographed series of stretching exercises design to increase body flexibility and moving more Prana/Chi/God life force throughout the human body, thus promoting longevity.

Kriya Dhyana Yoga Meditation: A highly structured series of seven meditations, designed to create control over the human mind, focusing the mind and bringing a sense of peace and well being to a person. These qualities lead to longevity in the human body.

Kriya Kundalini Pranayam(a): A highly structure breathing meditation with specific mudras (positions) that help facilitate performing it. This is a breath where they exhale is twice as long as the inhaling. This is something you would normally learn from a very advanced, Kriya Kundalini Yogi because it has critical elements necessary to properly perform it. Advanced practitioners of Kriya Kundalini Pranayam may take only one breath, every 25-45 seconds. Kriya Kundalini Pranayam should not be confused with Kundalini Pranayam, as there are differences in performing each. Twenty to thirty minutes of Kriya Kundalini Pranayam can lead naturally the breathless state of Samadhi. **People with heart problems are advised against performing Pranayam.** On the other hand, it could also rejuvenate your heart. **Use Kinesiology Muscle Testing to ascertain the course of action you should take. Caveat Emptor (buyer beware; use your own discretion)!**

Kriya Kundalini Yoga: An advanced and comprehensive system of Yoga, thousands, if not millions of years old involving Asanas (a series of stretching exercise), Dhyana (a series of structured meditations) and Pranayam (a) [a very structured breathing meditation

Maha Mrityunjaya Mantra: Another form of Sanskrit mantra/prayer devoted to the Sun God. It has the same body and mind-altering characteristics as the Gayatri Mantra. Refer to Gayatri Mantra for more info.

Prana: The same as Chi

Samadhi: The breathless state that can occur after doing a long session of Kriya Kundalini Pranayam(a) and in an advanced practitioner, it can happen spontaneously during the day. Not only does breathing stop or is severely limited, blood can stop circulating throughout the body, likewise. Samadhi leads a person to a euphoric state of being, wherein a person is in the brainwaves of deep theta and upper delta. Samadhi has **nothing to do People with heart problems are advised to refrain from Samadhi.** On the other hand, there could be untold benefits from doing this. **Use Kinesiology Muscle Testing to ascertain if this is the right thing for you. Caveat Emptor (buyer beware; use your own discernment)**

Soruba Samadhi: This is a full time state of Samadhi, wherein a person no longer needs to eat, drink or breathe, although they may choose to do so at times. The consciousness of someone in Soruba Samadhi is at the upper fourth and fifth dimensions and will work into even higher dimensions in many cases. A person in this state no longer becomes sick, does not age, and exhibits characteristic off less matter and more energy, wherein the appearance of their body is not highly defined. Said persons can project themselves about, here and there, at just below the speed of light.

Tai Chi Chuan: A relaxed way meditating while you are standing. It is thousands, if not million of years old in origin and is often a way where you can quickly build a lot of energy in the body, known as Chi, Prana or God life force. Please refer to chapter three of "A Map to Healing and Your Essential Divinity Through Theta Consciousness" for a complete description and diagrams, thereof.

The Bhagavad Gita: A famous subtext from *The Mahabharata,* which was about the travails and learning of Krish(a) and Arjun(a), fighting the forces of evil, 5100 years ago. *The Bhagavad Gita* is prized as a deep source of Kriya Kundalini Yoga, with insights contained only in one other classic Indian text, *The Yoga Sutras*.

Theta brainwaves: A brainwave between 4-7 Hertz and is attained in deep meditation, especially Kriya Kundalini Pranayam and times of intense dance, musical and sports performances. Tremendous relaxation is achieved as well as high creativity and complex problem solving.

Yagna: The fire associated with Prana and "The Intelligent Cosmic Vibration" and part and parcel with Agna.

Many references have been made to images and other resource works from which Dr. Newton has gleaned his wealth of knowledge. You are encouraged to tap into those items found on his website:

Other Books by the Author

Beyond the Mists of Time: When Trees Ruled the Earth And The State of Balance and Euphoria That Ensued There From

    Paperback and Kindle

    ASIN: 0996137122

    ISBN-13: 978-0996137126

The Hidden Codes of God: A Journey to the Unknown Secrets and Dimensions of the Divine and the Energy of Love

    Paperback

    ASIN: 0996137106

    ISBN-13: 978-0996137102

A Map to Healing and Your Essential Divinity Through Theta Consciousness: Physics of the Immortal "Light Body" and the Creator's Template of Perfection and Abundance for His People!

    Paperback

    ASIN: 145254445X

    ISBN-13: 978-1452544458

Pathways to God :Experiencing the Energies of the Living God in Your Everyday Life

    Kindle Edition

    ASIN: B00844NSIK

Thank you in advance for taking time to complete a fair and honest review in order that other readers, deciding whether they will fully enjoy their time reading *In Search of the Body Immortal*. It need not be long, and you can quickly complete the task at:

http://bit.ly/BodyImmortal_Review